MONA LISA

The Love Beyond Love

By
ButterflyMan

ButterflyMan Publishing LLC

Email: **contact@butterflyman.com**

Website: **www.butterflyman.com**

This book is a work of nonfiction.

All analysis, interpretations, and frameworks are the author's own.

First Edition — 2025

Printed in the United States of America

ISBN: 979-8-90217-011-2

Book Design: **ButterflyMan Publishing LLC**

LOVE BEYOND LOVE

Foreword :

The Love Beyond Love

There are loves that touch the skin.
There are loves that touch the heart.
And then, rarely — perhaps only once in a thousand lifetimes —
there is a love that touches the soul itself.

A love that cannot be bought, taught, trained, or imitated.
A love that does not belong to the world —
but reveals the world.

This novel tells the story of such a love.

It begins on a rainy afternoon in Paris.
Leonardo da Vinci, reborn in the modern age — a man carrying the quiet brilliance
of a thousand forgotten lifetimes — walks through Rue de Rivoli, unaware that
destiny is about to return to him the greatest secret he ever painted.

She appears not as a myth, nor as a masterpiece,
but as a woman with a gaze carrying centuries of silence.

Mina Lissa — the living echo of the Mona Lisa,
the soul he once captured but never touched.
She walks among the crowds unnoticed,
until the moment their eyes meet.

In that instant, time folds.
Not as magic — but as recognition.
The recognition only two souls of the same purity can feel.

He sees in her the quiet smile he once painted —
not on canvas, but in eternity.
She sees in him the creator who once saw her essence
before she existed as flesh.

It is not love at first sight.
It is love before sight —
a love carried across lifetimes,

beyond gender, body, desire, or possession.

They fall in love,
but what they fall into is not romance —
it is awakening.

A meeting of two beings who stand above tradition,
above norms, above labels,
refusing to reduce their connection
to anything the world can name.

This is a story of:
- The purity of soul meeting its equal
- The recognition between creator and creation
- The highest form of love — where kindness is effortless,
decency is natural, and affection is simply truth

Their love is not about being together.
It is about becoming whole.
It is not about possession, but revelation.
It is not about the world, but what lies beyond the world.

In a crowded modern Paris, amid noise, movement, and indifference, their
meeting becomes the one unrepeatable moment —
the moment that transforms two solitary lives
into a single, luminous truth.

A truth that cannot be sold, trained, predicted, or controlled.
Only found.

The love that da Vinci never lived —
and the love that Mona Lisa never received —
finally becomes real.

TABLE OF CONTENTS

CHAPTER LIST

PART I — THE AWAKENING

PART II — THE PAST REMEMBERS

PART III — THE BRIDGE BETWEEN LIVES

PART IV — COMPLETION

Chapter 1: Rue de Rivoli

Paris woke late that morning, wrapped in a thin, colorless mist that softened the hard edges of stone and glass. The light was pale, hesitant, as if the city were deciding whether to get up at all or turn over and sink back into its dreams.

On Rue de Rivoli, the traffic moved in uneven waves. Cars exhaled white ghosts into the cold air. Deliveries rattled over cobblestones. A bus stalled briefly at the light, its windows fogged from the warmth inside. Under the long arcade, shopkeepers pulled back metal grilles with scraping noises that echoed between the pillars.

Leon walked beneath those arches, coat buttoned up to his throat, scarf tucked in, hands deep in his pockets. The soles of his shoes made hardly a sound on the stone. He walked without hurry, but also without lingering, as if the rhythm of his steps were something the street already knew.

He liked this hour: after the street cleaners had passed, before the big tourist buses arrived, when the city still belonged mostly to people who lived in it. There was room in the air for thought. Room for the kind of silence that didn't demand to be filled.

Today, though, the silence felt different.

He noticed it first in his chest: not an ache, not a sharp pain, just a faint pressure, like the air before a storm. The feeling was subtle but persistent, a hand gently pressing against his sternum from the inside. He slowed, then stopped completely, standing between two colonnades and the black iron fence of the Tuileries Garden.

Beyond the fence, the trees stood bare, their branches fine and tangled against the gray sky. Puddles on the gravel paths reflected the skeletal rows, turning the garden into a sketch in ink and water. Someone was walking a dog near the central alley, the animal's fur matted with damp. The dog paused to shake itself, droplets scattering like a brief, private rain.

Leon closed his eyes for a moment and breathed in.

Wet leaves. Distant exhaust. A trace of roasted coffee, faint but distinct, drifting from some unseen café. The city was layered like a painting; he could almost feel each translucent wash laid over another.

The pressure in his chest grew more specific, less like weather, more like memory.

He opened his eyes and looked ahead toward the faint outline of the Louvre, its long façade stretching toward the horizon, windows still mostly dark. He had walked this route almost every working day for years. He knew the pattern of the stone, the rhythm of the traffic signals, the usual clusters of people even before they appeared.

Today felt misaligned, as if something behind the scenery had shifted by a fraction of an inch.

He started walking again.

At the corner, the wind turned, catching his scarf and lifting a strand of hair at his temple. He smoothed it back with an absent gesture and checked his watch, though he already knew he was early. The hands pointed precisely to eight-thirteen.

He should have felt the small satisfaction of being ahead of schedule. Instead, there was that strange pull again, not toward the museum doors but toward something less defined, like a sound too low to hear but impossible to ignore.

He had lived in this city for eleven years. Before that, Florence. Before that, Milan for a time, and Rome briefly, and a childhood in a smaller, unremarkable town he rarely thought about. His path had made sense, in its own quiet way: art school, apprenticeships, restoration labs, internships at minor museums, one fortunate recommendation that opened the door to the Louvre's conservation department.

He knew how he had come to this place. He just didn't know why, on this morning, it felt as though none of those choices had been entirely his own.

He stopped again at the pedestrian crossing opposite the museum. The glass pyramids rose in front of him, their surfaces catching what little light the sky offered. The main pyramid, with its clean lines and sharp edges, seemed almost indifferent to the surrounding historic mass of stone, but there was a balance there he had come to respect: the conversation between centuries.

The traffic light clicked to red. Cars rolled to a halt.

For a moment, everything held.

He felt it fully now, that pull, a thread drawn taut somewhere behind his ribs, extending outward through the glass and stone and crowds not yet arrived. The feeling wasn't urgent, but it had a kind of inevitability, the way one might feel a tide beginning to rise even while the shore was still dry.

He pressed a hand lightly against his coat, just below the collarbone, as if he might be able to smooth the feeling down. His fingers encountered just wool and the steady thump of his own pulse.

"You're getting sentimental," he murmured under his breath, the faintest hint of amusement in his voice.

The light turned green.

He stepped off the curb.

On the opposite side of the street, at almost exactly the same moment, a taxi door opened and a woman climbed out, tugging her bag after her.

Mina Lissa straightened, paid the driver through the window, and paused for a second to adjust the strap of her bag on her shoulder. The taxi merged back into traffic, leaving a line of pale exhaust in the air. She coughed once, reflexively, and then lifted her gaze.

From where she stood, the Louvre filled her field of vision: the spread of its wings, the symmetry of its courtyard, the cold clarity of the pyramid rising from the ground like a crystal tooth. She had seen it before, in photographs, in documentaries, on a brief teenage trip when everything had blurred together.

Today, it felt sharper.

The air was colder than she'd expected. She had checked the forecast before leaving Florence, but screens never quite captured the way cold in one city differed from another. Here, it felt crisp and direct, settling on the skin like a question.

She tightened her scarf around her neck and took a slow breath.

She had not planned this weekend. Three weeks earlier, she hadn't imagined being here at all. The tickets had been bought shortly after her last operation, during a lull between cases when exhaustion had washed over her—not the clean fatigue that came from physical effort, but the deeper, heavier kind that collected silently in the chest.

Her colleagues said she needed rest, a break, something to remind her that the world existed beyond operating rooms and consultations and hospital corridors. At first she had smiled and waved them off. The work was meaningful. That should have been enough.

Then, one evening, she had walked home through Florence's narrow streets, past stone walls still radiating the day's heat. She had caught her reflection in a shop window and seen someone precise, composed, and very, very tired.

On the impulse of that moment, she had gone upstairs, opened her laptop, and booked a flight to Paris. The hospital schedule contained just enough openness for a three-day trip. She didn't tell anyone until the tickets were confirmed.

Now she was here, bag on her shoulder, the taste of airplane coffee still lingering faintly at the back of her tongue, her body caught between the faded night of the plane and the gray morning of the city.

She should have felt excited. She felt instead a curious quiet.

She took a step toward the crosswalk.

That was when she saw him.

He was already halfway across the street, walking from the other side, his figure slight but steady, shoulders relaxed, his hands concealed in the pockets of a dark coat. There was nothing remarkable about him at first glance. He could have been a professor, a musician, a librarian, one of those people whose profession didn't leave obvious marks on their clothes.

It wasn't his face that stopped her. Not immediately. It was the way he moved.

His pace was calm, unhurried, as if he were in the right place at the right time and needed no more of the world than that. The crowds were thin, the cars held back by the light, yet he didn't appear to be taking advantage of the emptiness by rushing across. He let the space remain space.

She frowned, a faint line appearing between her brows. Something inside her tightened, the way muscles contract before a movement.

He lifted his head slightly and looked toward the museum entrance. The light caught the side of his face: a high forehead partially covered by hair that had silvered at the temples, a strong nose, a mouth that might have been quick to smile or slow to do so. Lines marked the skin around his eyes, but they were the kind carved more by concentration than by habitual frowning.

He was not beautiful, not in the way she would have described beauty in another context. He was striking in a subtler way, like a drawing that revealed more the longer one looked.

Then his gaze shifted, and their eyes met.

There was no thunderclap. No cinematic swelling of music, no sudden halt in traffic, no gasp from the city.

There was a change, quiet and distinct, as if someone had adjusted the focus of reality by half a turn.

Mina felt her breath catch. The air at the back of her throat thickened.

The look lasted barely a second. A passerby with a backpack cut across her line of sight, and then the man had reached the other curb. He didn't break stride, didn't look back, didn't do anything unusual at all. He simply walked on toward a side entrance where staff sometimes disappeared.

Her heart continued to hammer faster than it should have.

She told herself she was tired. Jet lag always made perception strange. Faces seemed familiar when they weren't. Streets felt distorted. The brain misfired briefly as it recalibrated to new time zones.

She stepped off the curb with the other pedestrians.

Still, as she watched the man from behind, something in the set of his shoulders, in the tilt of his head as he passed under the archway into the courtyard, seemed familiar in a way she could not place. She had the fleeting sensation one sometimes had when catching a fragrance that recalled childhood or a fragment of melody that evaded identification—recognition without context.

By the time she reached the main glass pyramid, the man had vanished.

She shook herself, shifted the weight of her bag to the other shoulder, and joined the line moving toward the security checkpoint.

It was nothing, she told herself.

Or it was something, but not a something that required explanation.

For now, there was the museum. There was the painting she had quietly wanted to see again, though she'd never admitted, even to herself, why it mattered.

Inside, the line moved slowly, but her thoughts moved slower.

Leon showed his ID card to the staff at the side entrance. The guard, a broad man with a sleepy expression, nodded and waved him through without much ceremony.

He descended a short flight of stairs and passed through a service corridor painted in a shade of beige designed not to be noticed. The air inside was warmer, filled with a mix of cleaning chemicals, old stone, and the faint smell of paper.

He greeted a colleague from another department, exchanged a few low, habitual phrases, and continued toward the conservation wing. The corridor turned twice, then spilled into a narrower hallway lined with unmarked doors. He stopped before one of them and unlocked it with a small, worn brass key.

The room inside was long and high-ceilinged, lit from above by a row of skylights that filtered the gray daylight. Worktables stood in orderly rows, each occupied by lamps, brushes, magnifying lenses, jars of pigment, and the various tools of their trade. A few canvases rested on easels, half-cleaned; others lay flat under protective cloths.

This early, the room was empty.

He set his bag down at his usual table and removed his coat, hanging it on the back of a chair. For a moment he stood still, listening to the silence.

It wasn't the same silence as outside. Here, it was layered with decades of murmured conversations, careful instructions, the scrape of chairs, the clink of glass. The memory of other restorers lingered in the room, the way the memory of previous hands remained in the surface of a painting even after centuries.

The pressure in his chest had eased slightly, but the sense of misalignment remained, as if his body were present but his attention lagged one step behind.

He looked at his schedule for the day, printed on a sheet of paper and pinned to the corkboard by his table: examine a small altarpiece with fresh cracks in the varnish, report on the stability of an early portrait's pigment layer, consult with another specialist about humidity control in one of the older rooms.

Routine tasks. Necessary. Precise.

He should have felt the calm of routine settle over him now, the familiar transition from the wide, diffuse perception of the street into the focused, microscopic mode of work. Instead, his mind kept circling back to the moment at the crosswalk.

The woman with the tired eyes and the dark hair gathered loosely at her neck. The way her gaze had met his, not in the curious, quick glance of strangers but with something else—something slower, deeper, as if she had paused inside herself to look.

He pulled out a chair and sat. For a while, he just looked at his hands resting on the table, as if they belonged to someone else.

The skin carried the faint stains of pigment that had never fully washed out, a subtle ghost of blue at the base of his thumb, a suggestion of umber in the fold near his index finger. His fingers were long, joints slightly pronounced, nails trimmed close.

He flexed them once, watching the tendons shift.

On another day, he might have gone immediately to his work, losing himself in lines and layers, in the delicate removal of dirt from an old canvas, in the satisfaction of revealing a color that hadn't seen the open air in a hundred years.

Today, he reached instead for the small sketchbook he kept in his bag.

It was nothing elaborate, just a well-worn book with off-white paper, its cover softened at the corners by long use. He opened it to a blank page, picked up a pencil, and, without planning to, began to draw.

At first it was just lines—curves, arcs, small decisions made almost without conscious thought. The movement of graphite over paper made a faint whispering sound in the quiet room. He felt his breathing slow, the world narrowing into the rectangle in front of him.

He didn't think of the woman as he drew. Or perhaps he did, but not deliberately. He thought instead in the language of planes and shadows, of the way light fell across a cheek, the way an eyelid folded, the direction in which a neck turned when someone was listening.

The outline of a face emerged quickly, then refined itself as if the pencil knew more than he did. A high forehead. A gentle slope of nose. Lips that were not full but had a certain softness at the corners. Eyes—not large, but deep, with a slight downward tilt that suggested thoughtfulness.

He paused and lifted the pencil, suddenly wary, as if he had stepped into a room he hadn't meant to enter.

He looked at what he had drawn.

The face on the page looked back at him with a calm, curious expression.

It was not exactly the woman from the street. It wasn't a perfect likeness. It was something older and younger at the same time, features smoothed by memory rather than sharpened by observation.

There was something else about it too—a balance in the proportions, a harmony in the relationship between eyes and mouth, jawline and cheekbones, that felt profoundly, unsettlingly familiar.

He turned his head slowly toward the far end of the room, where a reproduction of a famous painting hung on the wall: a simple print, placed there mostly as a joke by someone years ago. The image was so widely reproduced as to be almost anonymous now. People wore it on shirts, printed it on mugs, transformed it into memes.

The Mona Lisa smiled faintly from the cheap paper, her expression caught in that eternal uncertainty between amusement and resignation.

His gaze flicked from the sketch to the reproduction and back again.

No, he thought first. It wasn't the same. The woman he had drawn had slightly different features, a freer posture. The smile was less closed, less guarded.

Still. There was something in the eyes. In the composure. In the way the face seemed to be aware of something beyond the frame.

He shut the sketchbook with more force than necessary, the sound sharp in the quiet.

He told himself he was being ridiculous. He had spent years in proximity to that painting. It had seeped into his visual vocabulary the way a language seeps into a child raised among its speakers. Of course echoes would appear in his drawings. Of course his hand would, at times, unconsciously reproduce proportions it had been studying through microscopes and magnifying lenses.

He slipped the sketchbook back into his bag and stood up, telling himself firmly that he would think no more about it.

The feeling in his chest did not entirely agree.

In the main galleries, the day had properly begun.

Groups moved through the museum with uneven momentum. Some visitors flowed directly toward the famous attractions, their paths pre-determined by guidebooks and online lists. Others wandered more diffusely, drawn by color or curiosity.

Mina found herself carried along one of the broad corridors, then peeled off into a smaller room where a cluster of Renaissance paintings hung in ornate frames. She'd passed security, passed the ticket check, passed through the soaring entry hall with its grand staircase. Her feet had followed the general movement of the crowd, but her mind lagged behind, still at the crosswalk, still on the brief, inexplicable moment when her gaze had met a stranger's.

She shook her head lightly, as if to dislodge the thought, and focused on the nearest painting.

A woman in profile, hair elaborately arranged, her hands folded lightly in front of her. Another with a child balanced on her lap. A man with a serious expression, fingers resting on a book. The faces were both distant and intimate, their lives collapsed into a single pose, a single captured moment illuminated by careful light.

She leaned in closer to one, studying the texture of the paint, the fine cracks in the varnish, the way the surface caught the light.

It calmed her, the way a well-structured medical chart calmed her, the way a familiar procedure calmed her. The presence of order, of intention, of someone who had once stood in front of this same rectangle of space and thought: here, I will place a fragment of the world, and it will endure.

She moved from room to room like that for a while, letting images wash over her: saints and angels, mythological scenes, portraits of people whose names had long since lost their urgency but whose expressions still carried traces of private thought.

At some point, she glanced at a map and saw how close she was to the room that held the museum's most notorious resident.

She hesitated.

There was no reason not to go. It was almost obligatory. One did not come to the Louvre and ignore the Mona Lisa. Yet she had deliberately avoided heading there first. The last time she had seen it, in her teens, she'd been shoved and squeezed among a crowd of strangers all raising their arms above their heads, trying to capture the painting on screens instead of seeing it with their eyes. The memory of the jostling had smudged the memory of the painting itself.

But today was quiet still, not peak season, not peak hour. The crowd might be smaller.

She found her way to the correct staircase almost without looking at the map. Her feet remembered the route even if her conscious mind did not entirely.

The corridor leading to the room was already busier. Signs pointed the way. A few people hurried past her, their pace increasing as if drawn by anticipation.

She joined them.

At the entrance to the gallery, a guard watched the flow with practiced boredom. The room announced itself not by its architecture but by the density of bodies inside. She stepped through and felt the air shift from open to crowded.

The painting itself was smaller than most first-time visitors expected, hung alone on a special wall behind thick glass. A loose semicircle of people stood before it, phones and cameras in hand, an uneven halo of technology framing the old wood panel.

Mina moved closer slowly.

Expressions around her varied. Some people grinned, taking selfies. Some frowned, squinting behind their lenses. Others stared with a seriousness that might have been genuine contemplation or merely fatigue.

The glass reflected fragments of the room: silhouettes, colors, distorted shapes of faces. The painting sat calmly at the center of it all, unmoving, unchanged.

She waited for an opening and then slipped into a gap in the front line.

The noise dulled, as if sound itself had stepped back.

For a few seconds, the world narrowed to the oval of the woman's face, the dark fabric framing it, the hands folded with quiet assurance in the foreground. Behind her, that strange, improbable landscape of distant mountains and winding rivers stretched out, more dream than place.

Mina had seen the image in so many reproductions that seeing it here, in person, felt almost like seeing a friend after years of correspondence through letters. The familiarity was undeniable, but there was also a strangeness, a sense that the person behind the image might differ in subtle ways from the version she had constructed in her imagination.

She studied the eyes first.

They did not follow her, not literally, but there was a quality in them that suggested awareness, as if the woman behind them knew more than she said, more than she showed, more than anyone standing in this room could guess.

For a moment, Mina forgot the crowd.

She leaned forward just slightly, not enough to draw the guard's attention, but enough that her entire field of vision filled with the face and the faint, enigmatic curve of the mouth.

She had the sudden, irrational impression that the painting was looking directly at her. Not at the crowd, not at the general concept of "viewer" or "observer," but at her specifically, as if her arrival had been noticed and quietly acknowledged.

Her heartbeat quickened.

She told herself this was the familiar trick of a master composition. The angle of the eyes, the symmetry of the features, the subtle gradations of shadow—all pooled together to create the illusion of direct gaze. Many people likely felt this. It was part of the painting's enduring power.

But as she stood there, the sense of recognition deepened. It wasn't just that the painting looked at her. It was that the woman in the painting seemed, for the smallest fraction of a second, relieved.

The thought was so strange it almost made her laugh. She pressed her lips together, fighting an urge to step back.

The smile—that famously unreadable smile—appeared to soften. She knew, logically, that it hadn't changed. Her perception was shifting under the influence of her focus, of her mood, of whatever strange current had been running under her morning since the moment she stepped out of the taxi.

Still, the impression remained. The corner of the painted mouth seemed to dip slightly, not quite into sadness, not quite into joy, but into something like recognition.

Her chest tightened.

She imagined, absurdly, that if the glass weren't there, if the centuries between her and the painter's hand could collapse, she might reach out and the painted fingers would warm beneath her own.

A murmur from the crowd broke through her concentration. A tourist brushed her shoulder as they moved past, apologizing absent-mindedly in a language she barely registered. The spell snapped.

Mina stepped back.

From that distance, surrounded again by bodies and noise and the flicker of screens, the painting returned to its usual public self, the famous expression settling back into place like a mask. Whatever she'd thought she'd seen a moment earlier vanished, or hid, or retreated to a depth she could no longer access.

She left the room without looking back.

In the corridor outside, she leaned briefly against a cool stone pillar, drawing one deep breath, then another.

You are tired, she told herself. You are projecting. You came here with some vague idea that this trip would give you something you didn't know how to name, and now your mind is manufacturing significance out of harmless impressions.

Her pulse slowly returned to normal.

She continued through the museum, but her attention had lost its earlier clarity. Paintings blurred into one another. Sculptures lost their individuality. The rooms began to feel like variations on a theme rather than distinct spaces.

After a while, she checked the time and realized she hadn't eaten since a cramped breakfast on the plane. The idea of food suddenly seemed very important.

She checked the map again and found an exit near the Palais Royal. The cold air outside brushed her face, waking up the skin, making her nostrils sting a little. She crossed a small square, passed under another arcade, and stopped in front of a café whose windows glowed faintly yellow against the gray street.

Inside, the space was warm without being crowded. A few tables were occupied by people with laptops, a couple of tourists poring over a large map, an older man reading a newspaper so thoroughly he seemed part of the furniture.

She chose a small table near the window and took off her coat carefully, folding it over the back of the chair. Her body moved with the small efficiencies of habit: bag under the chair, phone placed face-down on the table, wallet ready for when the server came.

She ordered hot chocolate and a croissant when the waitress approached, then leaned back and let her head rest lightly against the wall.

The café smelled of coffee, baked butter, and something faintly sweet. Soft music played from somewhere near the counter, the volume low enough to be more atmosphere than sound.

Her eyes drifted to the window. People passed outside, heads bent against the cold, some talking, some alone, all wrapped in their own trajectories. The glass carried their reflections and also the faint echo of her own: a woman in her late thirties, hair loosely tied back with strands escaping, face marked by the subtle shadows of too many late nights at the hospital.

She looked at herself without judgment, or tried to. She was accustomed to thinking of bodies in terms of function: organs, systems, symptoms, healing. Beauty was something she noticed in others more easily than in herself.

When the hot chocolate arrived, she wrapped her hands around the cup and watched the steam rise.

She had come to Paris with no plan beyond this: to see one painting, to walk without needing to be anywhere at a specified time, to eat something not purchased from a hospital vending machine. She had expected perhaps a mild sense of relief. She had not expected... whatever the last hour had been.

The man at the crosswalk. The painting seeming to look directly at her. The feeling of being seen not as patient, not as doctor, not as passerby, but as something larger and quieter.

She lifted the cup and took a sip. The chocolate was thick, almost like melted dessert, sweet but with a depth that prevented it from being cloying. The warmth moved down her throat and settled in her chest.

The door of the café opened.

She did not look up immediately. A draft of cold air brushed across the floor, stirring her ankles, making the candle on the next table flicker. There was the sound of a chair scraping, the low murmur of a greeting.

Her gaze remained on the window for another second, following the movement of a bicyclist as he passed.

Then, without fully knowing why, she turned her head toward the door.

He was standing near the counter, speaking softly to the waitress, ordering something she couldn't hear. The same coat, the same scarf, the same slightly rumpled hair touched by gray. From this distance, she could see his face more clearly: the curve of his cheekbones, the way his lips moved around the French words, the line of concentration that appeared faintly between his brows when he listened to the waitress's reply.

Her fingers tightened slightly around the handle of her cup.

He turned with the small paper ticket for his order in hand and let his gaze travel across the room, searching for an empty table.

It caught on her.

For the second time that morning, their eyes met.

This time, neither of them looked away immediately.

There was no outward sign that anything extraordinary was happening. The background noise of the café continued: spoons clinking, pages turning, low conversations. Someone laughed briefly at a table near the back.

Yet, for the space of a few heartbeats, the air between them felt sharper, as if the distance had condensed into something almost tangible. Recognition moved across his face, not dramatic, but unmistakable. A slight widening of the eyes. A softening around the mouth. An almost imperceptible tilt of the head, the way one might make upon seeing someone one had been expecting without knowing their name.

Mina felt her own body respond before her mind found words. Her breath shortened. Her shoulders relaxed. Something deep in her abdomen tightened and then released, like a knot untangling.

She could have looked away. She should have, by all conventional rules of etiquette.

She didn't.

He took a step, then another, and chose a table two down from hers, close enough that she could hear the murmur of his chair against the floor. As he shrugged out of his coat, he glanced once more in her direction, as if to confirm that she was indeed still there, not an illusion created by his wandering thoughts.

She lowered her eyes then, not quickly, but gently, giving him his privacy and herself a moment to breathe.

Her heart was beating too fast again.

She placed her cup down, carefully, as if any sudden movement might shatter whatever fragile thing had just settled into the space.

In the small stretch of silence inside her mind, a thought rose, clear and unreasonable:

I have seen you before.

Not in this café, not in Paris, not in Florence. Not in any of the places she could name.

The feeling was older than memory, deeper than the usual tricks of the brain. It had the peculiar gravity of a dream that felt like a message rather than a random collage.

She kept her gaze on her hands, on the pattern of the ceramic cup, on the small ring of condensation the warmth left on the table. But in the corner of her eye, she saw him remove a notebook from his bag, open it, and sit for a moment looking at the blank page.

The waitress brought his tea. He thanked her, his voice low. The sound of it brushed against her like the touch of a sleeve in a narrow corridor—no more than that, but enough to make her skin aware of itself.

He didn't begin writing immediately. He held the pencil above the paper for a few seconds, hesitating, as if waiting for something to crystallize.

The logical part of her mind suggested that this was nothing more than coincidence. Two strangers who happened to share a route, a museum, a café. A city of millions produced such crossings every day. If she were to stand outside the hospital in Florence and watch people long enough, she would undoubtedly see the same faces pass by more than once.

That part of her mind was clear, rational, and disciplined.

It was also, at the moment, not the part making the decisions about where her attention went.

She lifted her gaze again, slowly this time, giving herself permission as though she were performing a delicate procedure.

He was sketching. The pencil moved in small, precise strokes. From her angle, she could not see the page clearly, only the motion of his hand, the way his fingers shifted for different lines, the way his wrist pivoted delicately.

He paused once, perhaps to examine what he had drawn, perhaps to correct something. His profile was turned slightly toward her. In that half-view, she saw not the stranger from the street but something else: a familiarity that made her think, absurdly, of the woman in the painting she'd seen earlier.

It wasn't that he looked like the painter in the old self-portraits she knew from books. It wasn't that he looked like any particular historic face. It was more subtle than that, something in the focus of his gaze, in the attention he gave to what was in front of him, as if the world, for him, existed in layers of light and shadow rather than in names and categories.

Her chest felt tight. She took a slow breath to loosen it.

He must have felt her watching, because he glanced up, meeting her eyes directly now, not by accident but with a quiet, questioning awareness.

She could have looked away again. She didn't.

"Bonjour," he said, almost apologetically, as if caught in the act of seeing her.

His voice had a soft roughness to it, not from disuse but from being used gently. The accent in his French was slight and hard to place, the kind that came from years of living in a place without having been born in it.

"Bonjour," she replied, her own accent more noticeable, Italian vowels slipping into the word.

His eyes lit with the small spark that appears when a puzzle piece finds its place.

"You're not from here," he said, then immediately looked faintly embarrassed. "Excuse me. That sounded—"

"No," she said, a hint of a smile forming without her permission. "I'm not from here."

He nodded, as if that made some private equation balance.

"Tourist?" he asked, softer this time, giving her the option not to answer.

"Short visit," she said. "From Florence."

"That's not far," he said. "But far enough."

Her smile widened by a degree. "You?"

"Here," he said, then seemed to realize how incomplete that was. "I mean—I live here. I work at the museum."

"The Louvre?" she asked, though the answer was obvious.

He nodded once.

The waitress appeared then to ask if she wanted anything else. The brief interruption broke the direct line between them. By the time Mina had declined and thanked her, the moment's intensity had softened to something more ordinary, more manageable.

She finished her hot chocolate slowly, aware of his presence next to her as one is aware of a painting hanging at the edge of one's vision. Not staring at it constantly, but feeling its shape in the room.

He returned to his sketch, but his eyes lifted now and then, almost shyly, as if he were checking to see if she still existed in the same space.

Outside, the mist had begun to thin. The light grew marginally brighter. People continued to pass by, umbrellas closed now, hats pulled down.

Inside the café, two strangers sat at neighboring tables, hands wrapped around warm cups, the distance between them unchanged and yet, in some quiet way, irrevocably altered.

Chapter 2: The Woman in the Crowd

The museum was louder in the afternoon. Leon felt it even before he re-entered the main corridors. Voices echoed off the stone walls—French, English, German, Mandarin, a few he couldn't identify. Shoes clattered across the floors. A group of students rushed past him, chattering, their backpacks swinging like pendulums.

He had returned to work after the café, but concentration refused him. He had stood at his table for almost fifteen minutes, trying to resume the standard rhythm of his tasks, but the precision of his hands was faintly wrong. Every familiar gesture seemed half a second delayed.

So he had stepped out into the museum proper, telling himself it was simply to stretch his legs, to clear his mind, to reset his thoughts. Yet the moment he entered the main wing, he realized he wasn't walking randomly.

His body moved with the quiet confidence of someone following footsteps already laid out.

He was heading toward the Denon Wing.

He didn't tell himself why.

The last time he had been inside the crowds surrounding the museum's most famous painting was months ago. Conservation work required him to see the Mona Lisa often—sometimes from less than a meter away—but that was in a controlled, private room. The public gallery was different: chaotic, noisy, heavy with heat and breath and the constant rise of phones.

He had always avoided it.

Now he walked toward it.

He kept his hands in his pockets, his shoulders slightly tense, not from cold but from anticipation he refused to name.

As he reached the landing of the staircase, the sound increased—people funneling into the gallery, guards giving quiet instructions, a low murmur of awe and disappointment mixed together.

The crowd was a living thing—shifting, pulsing, opening briefly, then closing again.

He stepped into the room.

For a moment, he didn't look at the painting.

He looked at the people.

Faces tilted upward toward phones. Parents telling children to hold the rail. A man complaining that the painting was "smaller than expected." A woman telling her partner to move a little more to the left for a better picture.

Nothing unusual. The same dance performed every day, thousands of times.

He scanned the crowd without meaning to.

His breath caught when he stopped.

She was there.

She stood on the right side of the semicircle, near the rope barrier, her posture calm among the restless bodies. Her coat was open now, the collar of her sweater visible, dark hair slightly frizzed from the humidity of the rooms. Her hands were not raised in front of her like the others; she wasn't filming or taking photos.

She was simply looking.

He felt something shift inside him again—not a dramatic sensation, not a revelation, just a small, firm click, like a gear settling into the correct position.

She didn't notice him immediately. Her attention was fixed on the painting, and he wondered what she saw. He watched her eyes trace the face, the background, the hands. She leaned in a little, the movement so subtle that others around her wouldn't notice, but he did.

She looked at the painting the way someone looks at another person.

He took a step closer.

Another.

The room felt suddenly narrower, the air warmer.

He stopped a few feet behind her, close enough to see the faint reflection of her silhouette in the protective glass. She tilted her head slightly to the right, and in that moment, for reasons he could not explain, he felt he knew exactly what expression would move across her face next.

A slight tightening of the lips. A barely perceptible narrowing of the eyes. As if she were trying to remember something she had never learned.

She exhaled slowly.

Maybe she sensed him. Or maybe she only sensed the change in distance, that delicate instinct humans carry from long-ago survival, the awareness of another presence behind the shoulder.

She turned.

Her eyes found him.

This time, the recognition was not a surprise. It was an acceptance.

The noise in the room seemed to fade—not disappear, simply fade, as if they had stepped into a pocket of quieter air.

He nodded once, the smallest gesture, not wanting to disturb the fragile balance of the moment.

She didn't smile. Neither did he.

It wasn't that kind of moment.

She took half a step toward him, then stopped, uncertain whether they had the right to speak in this place crowded with strangers.

He bridged the distance with a soft greeting.

"You left the café early," he said.

His voice was low, but she heard it clearly.

"I needed air," she replied.

She hesitated, then added, "And I wanted to see this again."

He looked at the painting briefly, then back at her.

"What did you see?" he asked.

The question surprised her. She blinked, then looked at the painting as if reevaluating it through his eyes.

"I don't know," she said after a moment. "Something... I can't explain. As if she wasn't just a painting today."

He didn't react visibly, but the words ran through him with the strange weight of déjà vu.

Most people spoke about the painting with clichés: mysterious smile, famous masterpiece, overrated, iconic, too small. Even the others in the room right now were commenting in those predictable categories.

Her description was different.

He realized then that he wanted to hear more.

He opened his mouth to ask another question, but a guard stepped closer, discouraging prolonged conversation near the front line.

She stepped back first, moving toward the side exit. He followed a few steps behind, as though the air had arranged the distance between them.

Once outside the room, she turned slightly toward him.

"I'm sorry," she said. "I didn't ask if you were busy."

He shook his head. "No. I can take a break."

They walked side by side down the corridor. The crowd thinned with each step until the sound of footsteps and whispering became easier to separate.

They reached a quieter hall lined with less famous works. A bench stood beneath a window that let in a soft, diffused light.

She stopped.

He stopped too.

For a moment, neither of them sat.

"What's your name?" she asked finally.

"Leon," he said.

"Mina."

He repeated her name once, quietly, as if pressing it into memory.

She sat then, and he took the other side of the bench, leaving a respectful distance but not so much that the space felt cold.

They both looked ahead at the painting opposite them—an early Renaissance portrait of a woman holding a book. It was calm, balanced, ordinary in its beauty.

Neither of them commented on it.

"You work here," she said, not as a question but as a way to begin.

"Yes. In conservation."

"That must be… peaceful."

"Most days."

She glanced at him with a small, attentive tilt of her head. "And today?"

He hesitated.

"Unusual," he said finally.

Her eyes lingered on him a second longer than politeness required.

"Me too," she admitted.

Silence followed—not awkward, but not comfortable either. It was the silence of two people listening to something inside themselves rather than the space around them.

He folded his hands loosely in his lap. She rested hers on the bench, fingers curled slightly inward.

"Why Paris?" he asked after a while.

"To rest," she said. "To breathe. To... I don't know. Reset something."

"Did it work?"

She looked down at her hands. "Not yet."

"And the painting?"

She looked up again. "That felt... different."

He nodded slowly, though he still chose his words carefully.

"It does that sometimes," he said. "To some people."

She watched him for a beat. "Is that what happened to you? The first time you saw it?"

He wasn't sure how to answer.

The first time he'd seen the painting—not the reproduction, not the image in books, but the real panel—he'd felt nothing dramatic. No electric shock. No spiritual awakening. Just a quiet, deep familiarity that had grown slowly over time.

He had convinced himself it was professional admiration.

Now he wasn't so sure.

Before he could form a reply, a group of visitors approached the same bench, chatting loudly in Spanish. Mina stood, giving them space. He followed.

"Are you staying long in Paris?" he asked.

"No. Two more days."

He nodded. "If you want to see the museum when it's quieter... I can show you some areas that aren't on the map."

She blinked, surprised by the offer. "Are you allowed to?"

He gave a small shrug. "Not officially. But I know when the crowds thin. The museum is different then."

She hesitated—not because she doubted him, but because she wasn't used to accepting invitations from strangers.

He sensed her hesitation but didn't withdraw the offer.

"You don't have to decide now," he said. "If you'd prefer to walk alone, that's fine."

He meant it.

She nodded once, acknowledging the sincerity.

"Maybe tomorrow," she said softly.

He accepted the answer with a simple dip of his head.

They stood there a moment longer, neither moving.

Then she spoke first.

"I should go. I promised to call a friend back home."

He didn't ask who. He didn't ask anything.

"Of course."

She paused, then: "Thank you... for saying hello."

He smiled faintly. "I didn't want to leave it at just the crosswalk."

Her eyes flickered with a kind of stunned honesty, as if someone had gently pressed a palm against a part of her she normally guarded.

She stepped back, then turned and began walking toward the grand staircase.

Leon watched her from where he stood.

He didn't follow.

He didn't call after her.

But his chest tightened again, that same quiet pressure from the morning, now sharper, clearer.

He remained there until she disappeared around the corner.

Only then did he exhale, long and slow, as if releasing something he hadn't realized he was holding.

Somewhere deep in the museum, a door closed with a soft echo.

He felt it.

But he didn't know why.

Chapter 3: Louvre at Night

The museum emptied slowly, the way daylight drains from a sky that cannot quite decide to be dark.

Leon watched it happen from his usual vantage points: the corridor outside the conservation wing, the small window that overlooked part of the main atrium, the staff staircase where the murmur of visitors' voices rose and fell with the hour.

Afternoons were always dense. The building swallowed thousands of footsteps, thousands of glances, thousands of small personal reactions that left no trace on the stone. But as the day moved toward evening, the weight of all that softened. Tour groups gathered for final counts. Guides closed umbrellas with a practiced snap. The last photographs were taken, the last comments made about sore feet and sore backs.

By six, the public side of the museum had begun to thin.

By seven, the tide had mostly receded.

Staff hours could stretch later. Conservators, archivists, administrators—there was always something more to finish, some report to send, some final adjustment to humidity settings, some small task that seemed easier to do when the air was quieter.

This evening, Leon stayed.

He told himself it was because his report on the Lombard altarpiece wasn't finished. The wording of his recommendation regarding the microcracks in the varnish still bothered him. He wanted to check one detail again before he sent it to his supervisor in the morning.

He could have done that tomorrow.

He stayed anyway.

By eight, most of his colleagues had left the conservation room. Coat sleeves brushed against chair backs, lights clicked off one by one, soft goodnights echoed briefly and then dissolved.

He remained at his table, the lamp above his work area casting a small circle of warm light onto the papers and tools.

The completed report sat in front of him, every sentence now clear, every detail checked twice. He had no more work to do.

He didn't move to leave.

The pressure in his chest had not disappeared after seeing Mina walk down the grand staircase. If anything, it had settled deeper, into a steadier, more persistent presence.

He closed the folder on the report and placed it neatly in the outgoing tray. Then he turned off the lamp above his table.

The room dimmed. Only the skylights and the emergency fixtures remained, a bluish twilight that flattened shadows.

He glanced at the clock on the wall. The red second hand moved with steady insistence. Eight thirty-two.

He picked up his key card and slipped it into his pocket.

At the door, he paused and switched off the remaining overhead lights. The room fell into a softer darkness, the shapes of easels and tables reduced to silhouettes.

He hesitated for a moment at the threshold.

Then he stepped into the corridor.

The museum at night was another building entirely. It held the same walls, the same frames, the same ceilings and stairways, but its pulse altered.

Without the constant friction of bodies and voices, the air settled. Sounds carried farther: the distant buzz of a cleaning machine, the click of a guard's shoes, the muted thump of a door closing two galleries away.

Leon walked with his badge clipped visibly to his jacket. The night security staff knew him well enough, but habit was habit. Rules existed to be observed.

"Bonne soirée, Monsieur Leon," one of the guards called from the end of a hallway.

"Bonne soirée," he replied.

"Late again?"

He shrugged. "Some days are longer."

The guard nodded with sympathetic understanding, the kind that crossed professions. "Don't stay until morning, hein?"

Leon managed a small smile. "I'll try."

He continued down the corridor, his steps slower now. There was no need for haste. The building belonged to a smaller number of people at this hour, and they moved through it with a shared, unspoken respect.

He wasn't heading directly anywhere.

Yet his path had a direction.

He avoided the most brightly lit routes, choosing instead side corridors where only a few lights burned overhead, spaced far apart. In these stretches, the paintings seemed closer, their colors richer in the pockets of illumination.

He passed a series of Italian works, their gilded frames catching the low light. He glanced at them in passing, their faces and gestures like old acquaintances he didn't stop to greet this time.

His feet knew the turns even when his mind drifted.

Down one staircase, along a hall, left at the familiar bust of an emperor whose nose had been carefully but unsuccessfully repaired sometime in the nineteenth century.

He reached a set of double doors and paused.

Beyond them lay the long approach to the room where the Mona Lisa hung.

He knew the painting was not there now. At night, for safety, it rested in a different space, monitored, secured, away from public reach. He had been in that room many times—sometimes for scheduled inspections, sometimes for adjustments to the reading of sensors, sometimes because the museum required certain rituals of reassurance after hours.

He could say he was only going to check a sensor reading.

He could say he wanted to verify a humidity level.

He could say many reasonable things.

He pushed open the doors.

The corridor beyond was almost empty of light. Only a few fixtures near the floor glowed softly, guiding a path without revealing much of what was around it. The walls retreated into darkness, the frames mere hints at the edge of vision.

His footsteps sounded louder here, despite the carpet runner laid along the center of the hall.

He passed the entrance to the public gallery where the painting usually hung behind its glass. The door was closed, the room within dark. He didn't look in.

At the end of the corridor, another security door waited.

He swiped his card, entered a code, and listened for the softened click of the lock releasing. The sound came, metallic but subdued.

He opened the door and stepped inside.

The private room was smaller than the public gallery, its walls plain, its contents controlled. Temperature and humidity monitors glowed quietly from their positions along the walls. In the center of the room, supported by a secure stand and surrounded by an invisible perimeter of alarms, the familiar wood panel rested, not facing a crowd now, but the empty air.

Here, the painting seemed smaller, more vulnerable.

Leon closed the door behind him. The mechanism sealed with a soft finality.

He didn't turn on the bright overheads. He activated only the side lights, enough to see clearly without transforming the space into a sterile lab.

Light fell gently on the woman's face.

He stood at a respectful distance, hands by his sides, and simply looked.

He had seen the painting so many times that each element should have been defined in his mind like the map of his own apartment. Yet there were always details that escaped complete containment: a particular curve, a subtle transition of tone, the suggestion that the smile might deepen or fade if one looked away then looked back.

Tonight, he didn't look analytically. He didn't parse brushwork or texture. He let his gaze rest the way one rests a hand lightly against a familiar door.

The feeling in his chest grew clearer in the painting's presence. It was no longer a generic pressure; it had a direction, a slight lean forward, like the impulse to step across a threshold.

He exhaled.

"You met her today," he said.

The sound of his own voice in the room startled him. He didn't usually speak here, not even to himself.

He felt foolish at once. He wasn't the kind of man who talked to objects.

But the sentence had come out anyway.

"You met her," he repeated, a little quieter.

He didn't know whether he meant the woman in the café or the woman in the portrait or both at once.

He took two steps closer.

From here, the detail of the cracking in the varnish was visible, the fine network that age had drawn across the surface. The pigments beneath remained stable, the result of careful layers and good materials. The hands, folded so calmly in the foreground, still held their weight with dignity.

Her gaze met his, as it always did.

He stared back, his mind emptier than usual. No analysis. No cataloging. No sorting through dates and provenance. Just the simple, unguarded act of looking.

Something moved at the edge of his perception.

At first, he thought it was the adjustment of his own eyes, the normal process of light recalibrating as the brain corrected for subtle changes. But the shift persisted.

The shadows around the corners of her mouth seemed to deepen by a fraction. The eyes... not changed, not in any way an instrument could measure, but there was a softening in them, a return of something he hadn't known was absent.

He took another step forward, then stopped himself so abruptly that his weight rocked slightly from heel to toe.

He knew very well that the painting could not move. He knew very well that the human eye, under strain and suggestion, created illusions. He had spent too many hours explaining that to others, calmly, logically.

Yet the sensation remained.

He felt watched, but not in the uncomfortable way of a guard's surveillance, not in the possessive way of someone staring too long across a room. This was quieter, more like standing in front of a mirror and realizing the reflection was not simply copying him, but observing him, making its own small decisions.

He laughed once, softly, to break the tension.

"Now I am definitely staying too late," he said.

He checked the humidity monitor. The readings were within safe parameters.

He checked the visual inspection log. Today's entries were all normal.

He lingered anyway.

Minutes slid by.

At some uncertain point, the edges of his awareness blurred.

The light in the room didn't change. The soft hum of the climate control system continued. But something in the way he felt his own weight on the floor shifted. His feet remained planted, yet the space between himself and the painting seemed to lengthen and fold at once.

The woman's face—familiar, famous, endlessly reproduced—grew clearer, not in detail but in presence. The background behind her darkened, the strange winding roads and bridges dissolving into a softer, hazier suggestion.

For a moment, it felt as though the painting fell away and only the person remained.

Not the sitter, not the model who had once held this pose centuries ago, but the person the painter had seen when he chose to paint her this way.

A warmth moved through his head, behind his eyes, like a tide pushing against the shore of thought.

He blinked.

The room dissolved.

Light came from a different source.

Not from electric fixtures behind frosted glass, but from a wide, high window half-covered by a curtain that filtered the sun into narrow bands. Dust motes danced in that light, turning slowly in the air like tiny, weightless planets.

He became aware of the smell of linseed oil, earth pigments, and something faintly metallic. The floor beneath his feet was wooden, uneven, marked by stains of paint and thinner.

He was standing before an easel.

The canvas—no, the panel—on it was half-finished. The outline of a landscape rose behind the vague suggestion of a seated figure. The face was still only sketched in, but the curve of the cheek, the line of the jaw, the tilt of the head were already there, waiting.

His hand held a brush.

He looked down at it, at the long, stained handle, at the tuft of bristles dipped in a dark, translucent glaze. His fingers were not quite his own. They were longer, thinner, the knuckles more pronounced, the nails stained with remnants of earlier colors.

He heard a sound behind him—the soft swish of fabric, the slight creak of a chair adjusting under a shifting weight.

"Maestro?"

The voice was gentle, with a muted warmth. Italian, but not from any modern city. The vowels carried a different weight, the consonants a different softness.

He turned.

A woman sat in the high-backed wooden chair a few meters away. Her hands rested loosely on her lap, fingers intertwined. Her dress was dark, the fabric heavy but well-made, with a bodice that shaped her posture without constricting it entirely. A veil covered her hair, tucked behind her ears.

Her face was younger than the one on the famous panel, not because of time but because the expression was less guarded. There was a directness in her gaze that would later soften into that famous ambiguity. For now, she was simply herself: thoughtful, curious, slightly amused.

She was not beautiful in the way poets described beauty, but there was a gravity to her presence that pulled the eye.

She watched him with a look he could not yet decipher, as if she were trying to decide something about him without letting him know.

"You stopped," she said.

Her voice carried the lightest suggestion of laughter.

He realized he had, indeed, frozen, brush in midair.

"Forgive me, Madonna," he heard himself say, and the sound of his own voice startled him. It was deeper, rougher, older than the one he used in Paris now. He felt the vibration of it in a different chest, a different set of lungs.

"Have I moved?" she asked.

"No," he said. "You have been... very still."

She smiled then, a small, private expression that began in her eyes and only reached her mouth a moment later. It was not yet the smile he would eventually capture, but it contained its seed.

His hand trembled.

He turned back to the panel, trying to steady his brush, but his focus kept splitting. Half of him noticed the way light fell on her hands, the exact shape of the shadow under her chin, the subtle color where her lower lip met the upper. The other half observed, with almost clinical clarity, that none of this should be happening.

He was dreaming. That was one explanation.

Another, less comfortable one lingered beneath it, like the darker layer of pigment beneath a translucent glaze.

"Is something wrong with the painting?" she asked.

He realized he had not applied a single stroke in the last minute.

"No," he answered slowly. "The painting is... fine."

"Then it must be me," she said. "Perhaps I am sitting badly. Tell me, and I will fix it."

There was no vanity in her tone, only a quiet willingness to collaborate in whatever he was trying to achieve.

He shook his head. "No. You are sitting very well."

She tilted her head a fraction, studying him with that same slight amusement.

"You look as if you have seen a ghost," she said.

He almost laughed. The impulse surprised both his present and whatever older self he was inhabiting.

"Not a ghost," he said. "Something else."

"Something worse?" she asked lightly.

"Something... more impossible."

She lifted one shoulder in the faintest shrug. "Then perhaps you should paint that instead."

He looked at her again.

Her face, her hands, her posture—everything felt known in a way that did not fit within the confines of this single studio, this single lifetime. It was as if he were seeing not only the woman in the chair but also versions of her layered through time, sitting in different rooms, wearing different clothes, existing in different languages.

He blinked.

The scene wavered.

For a moment, the light from the window and the light from the museum room overlapped, two realities failing to align. The smell of oil and pigment collided with the faint, clean scent of climate-controlled air.

He reached instinctively for something to hold.

His hand touched only the empty space in front of him.

The quiet hum of the monitors returned first.

The soft whir of the climate system followed.

His lungs pulled in a breath that tasted of filtered air and old stone.

Leon found himself standing once more in the private room of the museum, his hands by his sides, the painting in front of him unchanged, the woman's expression as calm and enigmatic as ever.

His heart pounded.

He took a step back, almost stumbling. His heel scuffed the floor.

The room was exactly as he had left it. No one else was there. The lights were the same. The monitors displayed their usual data.

Only his pulse refused to return to normal.

He raised a hand and pressed his fingers against his forehead. The skin felt slightly damp.

He tried to reconstruct the sequence of events: entering the room, standing before the painting, watching the light, feeling the strange slow tilt of the world, then— what? Falling asleep on his feet? Fainting without collapsing?

He glanced at his watch.

Eight forty-seven.

He had been in the room for less than fifteen minutes.

The vividness of what he had just experienced didn't fit inside that span. It felt longer, thicker, like time had expanded in one direction while contracting in another.

He looked at the painting again.

The face on the panel looked back with its usual calm. No trace remained of the life he had seen in that other room, under that other light. And yet, when he focused on the eyes, he felt a faint echo of familiarity, not as a conservator who knows every crack and pigment layer, but as someone who had once held a brush and attempted, with more or less success, to put that gaze into paint.

He swallowed.

"This is absurd," he said under his breath.

The painting did not disagree.

He checked the humidity reading again, partly for something practical to do, partly to convince himself that the world still followed its usual rules. Everything was normal.

He turned off the side lights, plunging the room into a deeper, cooler half-dark, then opened the door. The lock engaged behind him with its soft, definite click.

The corridor seemed narrower on the way back. The quiet felt heavier.

At the end of the hall, the guard from earlier was checking something on a handheld device. He looked up as Leon approached.

"Tout va bien?" he asked.

"Yes," Leon said. His voice sounded almost normal to his own ears. "Everything is fine."

"You look pale," the guard remarked, not unkindly.

"Too much artificial light," Leon replied. "I should go home."

The guard chuckled. "We all should."

Leon managed a thin smile and continued past.

By the time he reached the staff exit, the edges of what he had seen were already fraying. The details of the woman's dress in the studio, the exact sound of her voice, the way the dust had moved in the barred sunlight—those remained sharp. But the feeling underneath, the sense of inhabiting two selves at once, began to retreat, like a tide withdrawing quickly from shore, leaving only wet sand and a scattered line of shells.

He stepped out into the cold night.

The air outside felt different from the air inside, even though their temperature differed only slightly. The sky had cleared in patches, revealing a few dim stars barely visible above the city's glow. Streetlights pooled golden light onto the pavement. The glass pyramid in the courtyard reflected the darkness back at itself.

He walked along the edge of the building, hands in his pockets, collar upraised against the chill. His breath appeared briefly, then vanished.

One thought rose above the others, quiet but insistent:

He had not imagined the feeling in the café.

He had not imagined the pull at the crosswalk.

He had not imagined the strange, momentary change in the painting's expression when Mina had stood in front of it.

He could call everything else dream, stress, fatigue, a trick of a mind steeped too long in images. But those three moments aligned along a line he could not dismiss so easily.

He stopped on the pavement beside Rue de Rivoli, in nearly the same spot where he had stood that morning.

Cars moved past with a regular, indifferent rhythm. A bus rumbled by, interior lights illuminating the tired faces of passengers heading home. A couple walked past him, their hands linked loosely, talking quietly in a language he didn't catch.

He looked at the flow of traffic, then at the reflection of the museum windows in the dark glass of the bus shelter across the street.

He thought of Mina.

She was somewhere else in the city now—perhaps in a small rented room, perhaps at a restaurant, perhaps walking along the river. He didn't know. He had not asked. There would have been no reason to, not according to the usual rules strangers followed.

Yet he felt strangely certain that wherever she was, the day had unsettled her too.

He exhaled, a slow, measured breath.

Then he began walking toward home.

The night closed around him, not menacingly, but with a quiet neutrality, the way a canvas remains blank until someone decides to paint.

Behind his eyes, even as he walked, the image of the woman in the studio lingered: the way she sat, the way she smiled, the way she said, *"Perhaps you should paint that instead."*

The words followed him down Rue de Rivoli and into the narrower streets beyond, persistent as a half-remembered melody.

He didn't know yet what "that" was.

He only knew that whatever had begun that day had not finished when the museum doors closed.

It had only changed rooms.

Chapter 4: Echoes in Sleep

Paris grew quieter as the night deepened, each hour peeling away a layer of noise until only the bare frame of the city remained. Traffic thinned. Lights dimmed in apartment windows one by one. A soft drizzle began over the rooftops, turning the streets glossy and reflective, as if the city were trying to remember itself in the dark.

Mina had returned to her hotel in the early evening, a modest place on Rue Saint-Roch with narrow hallways and a view of a courtyard that held a single, stubborn tree. She had showered, changed into loose clothes, and forced herself to eat something. Her body accepted the food; her mind barely tasted it.

She had told herself she would read for an hour, maybe watch something mindless on her phone, but she had done neither. Instead, she had sat on the edge of the bed, elbows on her knees, hands pressed to her face, trying to steady herself.

The day had left her unmoored.

It wasn't only the man in the café or the museum—though that alone would have been enough to unsettle her. It wasn't only the painting, either. It was the quiet sense that the hours she had lived today did not belong entirely to the person she had been yesterday.

She felt stretched, as if her life, usually contained within the familiar boundaries of work and responsibility, had suddenly opened into a wider space she didn't yet know how to navigate.

Outside her window, rain tapped faintly against the glass.

She lay down eventually, turning onto her side, pulling the blanket around her shoulders. Her breathing slowed. Her mind drifted, disentangling itself from the day with the reluctant slowness of a ship pulling away from its dock.

Sleep came quietly.

And then—

Light.

Not the cold, artificial glow of a hotel lamp. Not the diffuse warmth of a Paris morning.

A different light, older, filtered through high windows in narrow shafts. Dust swirled slowly in it, graceful and unhurried, each particle floating as if obeying a rhythm too delicate for waking life.

She stood—not in her hotel room, not in any space she recognized.

The floor beneath her feet was wooden, uneven. She felt its texture. Her shoes... no. She wasn't wearing shoes. Her feet touched the grain directly, and the boards were cool, faintly rough.

She lifted her hands.

They were not her hands.

They were smaller. The fingers were slender, the nails short and clean, the knuckles soft. A thin gold ring circled one finger—not jewelry she owned, not a style she would have chosen.

Her breath caught.

A veil brushed her shoulders—a fine, delicate fabric she did not remember putting on. A gown fell around her body, heavier than anything she would wear now, the skirt brushing her ankles as she turned.

She turned slowly.

The room was a studio. Wooden beams crossed the ceiling. Against one wall stood shelves crowded with jars of pigment, brushes, bits of charcoal, and stacks of unfinished sketches. The smell of oil, earth, and something metallic filled the air.

An easel stood before her.

Behind it—someone was painting.

She couldn't see the painter's face at first; he leaned toward the canvas, intent on a detail near the woman's right eye—the eye that was hers, though she did not remember posing for this.

She stepped closer.

Wood creaked beneath her feet, the sound sharp in the quiet.

The painter looked up.

She stopped breathing.

He was younger than the man in the museum, younger than Leon—yet she knew him. Not from the present. Not from Paris. Not from any memory she possessed consciously.

She knew him the way one recognizes a melody heard once long ago, the way muscles remember a movement the mind has forgotten.

His face was leaner, the lines around his eyes softer but still present, the expression familiar even though the era stamped itself in every detail of his clothing, his tools, the trimmed beard at his jaw.

His gaze met hers with an intensity that did not startle her. It felt expected.

"Sei stanca?" he asked gently.
Are you tired?

His voice carried warmth, familiarity. The cadence of it pulled at something deep inside her, something she had no name for.

She tried to answer.

Nothing came out.

He set the brush down carefully, wiping his fingers on a cloth with habitual, unthinking precision. He stepped closer, not touching her, but with the ease of someone who had stood beside her many times before.

"You can rest," he said. "The light is fading anyway."

His Italian was old, softer, more textured than the language she spoke now. Yet she understood him perfectly.

She looked at the panel on the easel.

She saw herself—not herself as she was, but herself as this other woman. The tilt of the head, the faint suggestion of a smile not yet fully formed, the eyes looking out with that quiet, unreadable expression.

Her throat tightened.

He noticed.

"You seem troubled," he said softly. "Sit. Stay a moment."

He moved one of the chairs closer for her, the scrape of its legs a strangely comforting sound.

She sat automatically.

Her hands—those unfamiliar hands—rested in her lap again, fingers intertwined.

He studied her quietly, not in the way a doctor might examine a symptom, not in the way a stranger might size up another, but in the way someone reads a beloved book, page by page, layer by layer.

"What makes you uneasy?" he asked.

She opened her mouth.

This time, sound emerged.

"I don't know," she whispered.

Her voice was not the one she used in operating rooms, nor the one she had used with him in Paris. It was younger. Softer. Foreign and familiar at the same time.

"You will tell me when you do," he said with quiet certainty.

She looked at him—really looked—and a wave of recognition moved through her so sharply she clutched the fabric of her skirt to steady herself.

He stepped back to the easel then, adjusting the panel's angle, testing the surface with the back of his fingers.

A warmth spread at the base of her spine, a sensation of falling not downward but inward, as if she were descending into herself.

Her breath quickened.

The room trembled, just slightly, like a reflection rippling on water.

She reached out instinctively, gripping the arm of the chair.

The painter turned sharply.

"Mina?"

Her eyes widened.

He had not said her name.

Yet she heard it.

The scene flickered.

The light fractured.

Her heartbeat roared in her ears.

The room collapsed around her like wet paper.

She woke with a sharp inhale.

The ceiling above her was smooth, white, modern.

Her hands—her hands—were clenched in the blanket.

Her chest rose and fell rapidly, as if she had run up a flight of stairs.

Rain tapped steadily against the window.

She pressed a shaking palm to her forehead. Her skin was damp. A faint imprint of the dream lingered behind her eyelids—the rough wood of the studio floor, the dust in the sunlight, the weight of the gown, the brush in his hand, his voice, his face—

Her heart clenched painfully.

She sat up slowly, legs over the edge of the bed, feet on the carpet. Her breath settled in short, uneven waves.

It wasn't a normal dream.

She had normal dreams—chaotic, fragmented, nonsensical. Slices of the day mixed with forgotten memories. Bodies without faces. Rooms that didn't exist.

This had been different.

Coherent.

Weighted.

It felt as though she had lived it, not imagined it.

Her fingers brushed her hair back behind her ear, trembling slightly.

She whispered into the empty room, without intending to:

"What is happening to me?"

She didn't expect an answer.

The silence that followed felt heavier than before, as if the echo of the dream pressed against the walls, shaping the space around her.

Her gaze drifted toward her coat draped over the chair.

Inside the pocket was the café receipt she had crumpled absentmindedly hours earlier.

A small corner of the paper peeked out, pale in the darkness.

Her throat tightened.

She thought of him—the man she had met by accident, twice, in one day. The man whose eyes had unsettled her in a way she had not been unsettled in years. The man who looked at art the way she looked at anatomy—with reverence, with discipline, with something deeper underneath.

She rose from the bed and walked to the window, pulling the curtain aside.

The courtyard below glistened in the rain.

Somewhere in the city, he was awake or asleep, walking home or already home, unaware of the strange dream that had woven itself into her night.

Or perhaps not unaware.

The thought sent a shiver down her spine.

She placed her forehead lightly against the cold glass.

Tomorrow, she would see him again.

She didn't know how she knew it.

She just did.

The rain continued, steady, insistent, tapping against the window as if trying to speak in a language older than memory.

She closed her eyes.

And the painter's voice—his other voice—echoed softly in her mind:

"Tell me when you know."

The sound faded slowly.

But the feeling remained.

It did not let her sleep again.

Chapter 5: The Day After

Morning came slowly, as if the light were reluctant to enter her room.

Mina sat on the edge of the bed long before the alarm she had set. She had slept little, if at all. Each time she closed her eyes, fragments of the dream returned—not as images this time, but as sensations.

The weight of the gown on her shoulders.
The faint scent of linseed oil.
The warmth of his gaze when he looked up from the easel.

None of it dissolved the way dreams usually did. It clung to her like perfume on fabric.

She rose, washed her face, dressed with automatic motions, and left the hotel with a quiet urgency she tried not to name. The morning air was cold enough to make her eyes water. A bakery on the corner pulled warm bread out of steel ovens, and the smell briefly cut through the fog in her mind.

She didn't buy anything.
She wasn't hungry.

She walked toward the Louvre almost without thought.

Leon had also slept badly, but for different reasons.

He woke twice in the night, once with his hand pressed against his chest, once with his fingers curled as though gripping a brush he no longer held. The dream—the memory or hallucination or whatever name he refused to choose—had faded in its visuals but not in its substance. He could still feel the inside of that studio, the breath of another century.

He had gone to work early, arriving when the halls were still cold and the cleaners were mopping the marble floors. In the conservation room, he turned on the lamps and sat at his table, staring at the tools laid out before him.

He could not bring himself to pick any of them up.

Instead, he opened the sketchbook.

The portrait he had drawn yesterday—the one that resembled her without being exactly her—stared back at him.

He touched the page with the back of his knuckle, a gesture so gentle it surprised him.

He closed the book.

At nine-thirty, the staff rooms buzzed with routine. He forced himself to walk toward the administrative meeting he was scheduled to attend but stopped halfway down the corridor.

He turned around.

He didn't want to see the painting again.
Not yet.
Not with the night still clinging to him.

He walked instead toward the public galleries.

Mina reached the museum courtyard with hands slightly numb from the cold. She had walked faster than she realized. The line to enter had not yet grown long. She joined it, heart beating with a quiet, insistent rhythm.

She didn't know if he would be here.

She didn't know if she wanted him to be.

When the doors opened, she moved with the first wave of visitors, feeling both self-conscious and foolish for scanning every corner, every staircase.

She turned into the Denon Wing without deciding to.

The steps felt familiar.
Too familiar.

She reached the landing.

She paused.

For a moment she thought she was mistaken—another man standing with his back to her, hair slightly longer, posture similar.

But when he turned, she knew.

He saw her at the same instant.

Neither of them smiled.
Something in the air between them made smiling feel too small.

He walked toward her, slow, steady steps, as if approaching something fragile.

"You came early," he said.

His voice was soft, careful.

She nodded. "I couldn't sleep."

He didn't mention dreams.
She didn't either.

Visitors pushed past them, but it felt as if they were standing in a space slightly outside the main flow of the museum.

"Do you want the quiet tour?" he asked.

She nodded once.

He motioned for her to follow.

He led her through a side corridor, one that most tourists overlooked. The lighting was dimmer here, the ceilings lower, the air cooler. Their footsteps echoed softly on the polished floor.

"These halls are older," he said. "They creak. They sigh. They hold on to stories."

She listened—not only to his words but to his voice, its restrained cadence, as if he were accustomed to talking to paintings rather than people.

He unlocked a small door.

"This gallery isn't closed," he said. "It's just forgotten."

Inside, the room was long and narrow, lined with works that had fallen out of fame—portraits of minor nobles, studies of landscapes, religious scenes once beloved and now almost invisible to the world.

There were no people here.

The quiet pressed softly against them.

Mina stepped closer to an old portrait of a young woman in profile. The paint had darkened over time, but the delicacy of the features remained. The woman's expression was serene, almost inward-turning.

"She looks like someone who knows a secret," Mina said.

Leon didn't answer immediately.

Instead, he stepped beside her, studying the portrait with the kind of attention he reserved for things that mattered.

"The painter knew her," he finally said. "Not just her face."

"How can you tell?"

"Because he painted her as if he were remembering her, not observing her."

Mina turned her head slightly, looking at him instead of the painting.

She hadn't known that was something one could see. But the moment he said it, it felt undeniably true.

He didn't look at her. His gaze was on the portrait. But his presence beside her felt calibrated, attuned, as though he were aware of her breathing, steadiness, the shift in her weight from one foot to the other.

She looked away first.

"Was there someone you painted like that?" she asked quietly.

He stiffened.

For a heartbeat, the museum felt too still.

He finally answered, "No. I've only restored paintings. Not created them."

"You draw."

He blinked. "How do you know that?"

"In the café."

He nodded once, as if remembering.

"I'm not an artist," he said. "Not really."

She didn't contradict him, though the sketch she had glimpsed on his page—only a blur from her angle—had left a faint impression of grace.

They walked through three more small galleries. He pointed out small details she would never have noticed: a fingerprint trapped in centuries-old varnish, a faint underdrawing visible only at an angle, a correction in the paint where the artist had changed his mind about the tilt of a hand.

He spoke without performance, without ego. The knowledge flowed out of him like something he didn't control. She listened quietly, the rhythm of his explanations calming something unsettled inside her.

After nearly an hour, they returned to a main corridor.

The noise of the larger museum surged back, filling the space with a brightness that felt intrusive after the long, quiet halls.

Mina paused at the top of a staircase.

Leon stopped beside her. The crowd continued around them.

He looked as though he wanted to say something but was choosing his words with unusual caution.

She turned toward him. "You felt something yesterday. Didn't you?"

His jaw tightened.

"Yes," he said. "I did."

"In the painting room?"

He looked sharply at her.

"How do you know that?"

She hesitated. Her hands tightened slightly on the strap of her bag. "I had a dream."

She said it simply, without trying to soften the strangeness of it.

He studied her expression, searching for hesitation, uncertainty, exaggeration. He found none.

"What kind of dream?" he asked.

She inhaled slowly. "A studio. A chair. A... painter."

The last word trembled slightly in the air.

Leon's pulse quickened.

He took a step closer—not enough to startle her, not enough to break propriety, just enough that the distance between them grew charged.

"What did he look like?"

She shook her head. "It wasn't clear. Or maybe it was too clear. I don't know. It felt like... I was someone else."

His breath left him in a slow, steady exhale.

She lifted her gaze to meet his. "You felt it too," she whispered.

He didn't answer.

He didn't have to.

The museum noise seemed to dim again, the way it had yesterday when their eyes met in the painting room.

Something fragile and enormous stood between them, something neither of them had language for yet.

Mina swallowed, her voice barely above a breath.

"What is happening to us?"

Leon shook his head once—small, helpless.

"I don't know," he said honestly. "But it began before we met."

A shiver moved through her.

He looked at her as if she were light itself.

She turned slightly, not stepping away but grounding herself.

"Can we walk?" she asked.

She didn't explain why.

He didn't need the explanation.

They walked side by side through the museum, neither speaking, both aware that something had shifted in the air between them—something delicate, something undeniable, something that felt older than the building they stood in.

When they reached the exit, the winter light outside had grown brighter, reflecting off the wet pavement.

They stopped just under the arch.

She looked at him.

He looked at her.

Neither of them knew what the next step should be.

Neither of them turned away.

Rain began again, a soft, fine mist drifting sideways in the wind.

She spoke first.

"Tomorrow?" she asked.

His answer came without hesitation.

"Yes."

She nodded once, then stepped into the rain, disappearing slowly into the moving crowd, her silhouette absorbed by umbrellas and coats and the pale gleam of wet streets.

Leon watched her until she vanished.

Only then did he whisper to himself, without intending to:

"This is not chance."

But the wind carried the words away before they could reach the stones beneath his feet.

Chapter 6: A Breath Between Days

The rain softened by late afternoon, turning into a thin mist that clung to the city like a fine veil. Paris became muted—edges blurred, colors subdued, sounds softened. It was the kind of weather that made everything appear slightly dreamlike, as if the day were happening behind glass.

Leon did not go straight home.
He walked.

Not with purpose, but with a restlessness pulsing beneath the surface of his thoughts. He moved through the narrow streets behind the museum, past bookstores with fogged windows, cafés humming with late afternoon conversations, the faint clatter of plates being stacked in preparation for the dinner rush.

He wasn't thinking—
or rather, he was thinking so much that none of the thoughts could take shape.

Every few minutes, the same image floated back to him:

Mina, standing at the top of the staircase, her eyes steady and searching as she whispered, *"You felt it too."*

He had tried, at first, to rationalize everything. But each attempt dissolved before it fully formed.

Coincidence didn't explain the dream.
Fatigue didn't explain the studio.
Memory didn't explain the way she looked at him, not as a stranger, not as a visitor passing through, but as someone who had stepped into her life from a place older than their own names.

He turned a corner and found himself along the Seine. The river was gray, restless, carrying the mist across its surface like drifting breath. He leaned against the stone railing, watching the small waves break irregularly against the embankment.

He closed his eyes.

The scent of rain.
The faint metallic tang of the river.
A distant church bell.

The soft echo of footsteps from passersby.

And beneath all of it, that same internal hum—
the sense of something moving under the surface of his mind, like a memory rising from deep water.

When he opened his eyes again, evening had begun to gather along the rooftops.

He pushed himself away from the railing and made his way toward the Île de la Cité, weaving through the quiet streets until he reached a small square where an old tree grew, its branches heavy with moisture. A kiosk stood nearby, the vendor closing down for the day, stacking unsold postcards into neat bundles.

Leon sat on a bench and rested his elbows on his knees.

For a while, he simply breathed.

There were moments in life one recognized as turning points only long after they had passed. And then there were moments like this—quiet, ordinary on the surface, but carrying a weight that pressed into his bones.

He knew, with a clarity that scared him, that he had already crossed a line. There was no stepping back.

He checked his watch.

The hour was later than he thought.

He stood, pulled his coat tighter, and began the walk home. The rain had settled into a fine drizzle by the time he reached his apartment. He climbed the stairs slowly, the air in the building thick and still. When he entered, he didn't turn on the main light. He removed his coat and shoes and sat at the small table in the kitchenette, staring at the blank page of his notebook.

He picked up his pencil.

He drew without thought.

Light strokes at first, then bolder ones. A jawline. A curve of cheek. A shadow beneath the lips. Each line steadier than the last. When he pulled back, he saw not a portrait but a gesture—an impression of her, not exact, but unmistakable.

The pencil dropped from his hand.

He pushed the notebook away and exhaled sharply, as though he had been holding his breath for too long.

He turned off the lamp.

He did not sleep for a long time.

Mina walked without aim as well, though she did not cover as much ground. She lingered in small streets near her hotel, stopping occasionally beneath the overhangs of storefronts to watch the rain gather and slide off the edges in narrow streams.

Her dream clung to her.

But it was not the dream itself that unsettled her most—it was the way her body remembered it. The weight of the gown. The sound of the painter's voice. The sense of being observed not as a stranger, nor as a doctor, nor as a woman of her age and profession—
but as someone held in a gaze that recognized her completely.

She stopped near a florist's shop, its windows streaked with condensation. Bouquets had been placed in buckets outside, despite the weather—white lilies, pale roses, eucalyptus branches still beaded with rain.

She lifted one eucalyptus stem and brought it to her nose, inhaling slowly. The scent was sharp, cleansing, familiar. For a brief second, it steadied her.

Inside her coat pocket, she felt the crumpled café receipt.
She removed it slowly.

On the back of it, faint pencil marks crossed the paper—an accidental impression, the pressure transferred from the page he had been sketching on above it.

Barely visible.
But real.

Her breath caught.

She folded the paper carefully and tucked it into her wallet, as though it were something fragile.

When she returned to the hotel, the lobby was warm, the air humming softly from the radiator. She nodded to the clerk at the desk, took the small elevator to her floor, and stepped inside her room.

She closed the door behind her and leaned against it.

Her throat tightened unexpectedly.

It wasn't loneliness.

It wasn't fear.

It was recognition—
the recognition of a sensation that had no place in her life before yesterday.

She removed her coat, draped it over the chair, and sat on the edge of the bed, hands clasped loosely in her lap.

She whispered into the quiet room:

"This is not possible."

The room did not answer.

She reached for the bedside lamp and turned it off.

Darkness settled softly around her.

She lay down, facing the window, watching the faint glow of the courtyard rise and fade as the clouds passed overhead.

She didn't sleep.

But she didn't resist the quiet, either.

She let it settle over her like dust settling across forgotten pages.

When dawn finally touched the edges of the sky, she had not moved from where she lay.

But something inside her had.

She felt it—
not a change, not yet, but the preparation for one.

And when she finally closed her eyes, just for a moment, she saw again the painter in the studio, the brush lifted, the gaze steady, and the slight smile beginning to form on his face.

Not for the painting.
For her.

And her body reacted with a quiet shudder, like a chord struck in a long-silent instrument.

Leon dreamed lightly near morning.

Not the studio.
Not the woman in the chair.

Just a voice.

Soft, low, nearly a whisper.

"Domani."

Tomorrow.

He woke with a start.

And for the first time in years, he didn't question whether the voice was his imagination.

He already knew what tomorrow meant.

Chapter 7: The Meeting on Pont des Arts

Morning broke with a pale, washed-out light, the kind that revealed every detail of the city without offering warmth. Paris looked softer under it, as if the buildings themselves were waking reluctantly, blinking away a long night.

Mina left the hotel before breakfast.

She walked slowly at first, as though waiting for her body to settle into the rhythm of the day. Her hands were tucked into the pockets of her coat. The cold seeped in gradually but did not push her back indoors.

The sky above the Louvre was a dull silver when she reached the courtyard. Crowds had not yet gathered—just a scattering of early visitors, a few joggers passing through, and museum staff heading toward the staff entrance.

She did not go inside.

She waited.

She didn't send a message.
She didn't even know if he had a number she could write to.

But deep inside, beneath her caution, beneath the rational layer of her mind, a quiet certainty whispered that he would come.

And then he did.

He crossed the courtyard from the opposite side, his coat unbuttoned, scarf tucked loosely around his neck. His gait was deliberate, almost hesitant, as if part of him questioned his own presence there.

When he saw her, he slowed—not from surprise, but from recognition. A look flickered across his face: relief, quiet intensity, something like inevitability.

He approached her.

They didn't greet each other with a handshake or the usual pleasantries. The moment didn't allow such distance.

"Good morning," she said, her voice steadier than she felt.

"Good morning," he replied.

There was a pause—
not awkward, not empty, but charged, as though the air between them needed a moment to adjust.

"Walk with me?" he asked.

She nodded.

They left the courtyard and headed toward the river. Their steps were unhurried, synchronized without effort. They walked past the Palais Royal side street, where bakeries were setting out trays of warm pastries, and turned toward the Pont des Arts—the pedestrian bridge that stretched lightly over the Seine, its thin wooden slats still damp from the night rain.

When they reached the center of the bridge, Mina stopped.

The river flowed beneath them in slow, heavy movements, its surface shifting in long ribbons of gray-green. On the opposite bank, the dome of the Institut de France rose against the morning sky, solemn and perfectly balanced.

Leon leaned his hands on the railing, releasing a long, slow breath.

For a moment, neither of them spoke.

The quiet was not the quiet of strangers searching for words—
but the quiet of two people circling a truth they were not ready to touch directly.

Mina turned to him first.

"You said yesterday it began before we met," she said. "What did you mean?"

Her voice held no challenge—only the need for clarity, for honesty.

Leon didn't answer immediately. His jaw tightened slightly, as if he were weighing the shape of his thoughts before offering them aloud.

"I don't know when it began," he said slowly. "But it didn't start at the museum. Or the café. Those moments felt like… recognition, not discovery."

She felt her pulse quicken.

"Recognition of what?" she whispered.

He shook his head. "That's what I'm trying to understand."

A gust of cold wind swept across the bridge, carrying the distant sound of a boat engine starting. Mina turned her face slightly, letting the wind brush past her.

"I had another dream," she said quietly.

He closed his eyes briefly, as if bracing for something he already knew would matter.

She continued.

"It wasn't chaotic. It wasn't like a normal dream. It felt like…" Her voice thinned. "Like I was remembering something. Something that didn't belong to me."

Leon's fingers tightened around the railing.

"A studio," he said before he could stop himself. "Light from a high window. Dust in the air."

Her eyes widened. "Yes. Exactly."

"And a woman sitting for a painter," he said.

Her breath caught in her throat.

"Yes."

They stood in silence, the truth of their shared vision stretching between them like an invisible thread.

He didn't ask her what the painter looked like.
She didn't ask him what the woman resembled.

Some knowledge lived beneath the surface of their consciousness—
not yet named, not fully understood, but undeniable.

Mina pressed a hand lightly against her chest, fingertips brushing the fabric of her sweater.

"I've never felt anything like this," she said.

"Neither have I."

A faint tremor ran through her voice. "It frightens me."

He turned to her then, fully, not just with his gaze but with the quiet solidity of his presence.

"I'm not here to frighten you," he said.

"I know," she whispered. "That's the strange part."

He exhaled, his breath visible in the cold air.

"When I look at you," he said softly, "there is a sense of... familiarity I can't explain."

She swallowed. Her pulse hammered.

"In the dream," she said, "the painter—he looked at the woman with a kind of... recognition. Like she was someone he already knew, not someone he had just begun to paint."

The same recognition passed across Leon's face.

"And the woman," he asked quietly, "how did she look at him?"

Mina hesitated, her gaze drifting toward the water.

"As if she trusted him," she said. "Completely. Without question. As if they had lived that moment before."

Her voice trembled at the last words.

Leon's breath faltered.

The wind rose softly, brushing across their coats.

He lifted a hand to the railing, then let it slide down, slowly, until his fingers hovered an inch from hers—not touching, but close enough that her body felt the heat of his skin.

She didn't move away.

Her eyes met his.

For a suspended moment, the present seemed to overlap with something older—something not fully remembered but deeply felt.

It wasn't romantic tension.
It wasn't desire.
It was recognition—pure, overwhelming, and inexplicable.

Mina looked down at the space between their hands.

Then she whispered something she had not intended to say:

"Why does it feel like I've lost you before?"

Leon inhaled sharply.

His eyes closed, as though the question pierced a place inside him that had lain dormant for years.

He spoke with a voice barely above the river's murmur.

"Because that's how it feels to me too."

Her lips parted.

He finally let his fingers touch hers—just the slightest brush, like the beginning of a signature written in air.

The contact was brief—fleeting, delicate—but it sent a ripple through both of them, subtle yet unmistakable.

She drew in a soft breath.

He opened his eyes.

Their hands separated almost immediately, but the echo of that touch lingered, warm and unnerving.

The river flowed calmly beneath them.

People passed behind them on the bridge, their footsteps muted on the damp wood.

Neither Mina nor Leon spoke for a long moment.

Finally, Leon straightened slightly, grounding himself.

"Mina," he said quietly, "what we're experiencing—whatever it is—it's not random."

Her eyes lifted to his, steady and certain.

"No," she agreed. "It's not."

He stepped back half a pace, not in retreat but in an attempt to steady the fragile balance between them.

"There's something we haven't faced yet," he said. "Something behind all of this."

She nodded, her breath unsteady.

"I know."

He watched her carefully.

"Do you want to keep going?" he asked.

It wasn't a casual question.
It wasn't about the walk or the conversation.
It was about stepping into something neither of them understood fully, something that had already begun unraveling the quiet structure of their lives.

Mina looked out toward the river, the mist drifting above its surface.

Then she turned back to him.

"Yes," she said.

The slightest relief crossed his features.

He moved to stand beside her again, without touching her.

"Then we go slowly," he said.

Her voice softened.

"Together?"

He nodded once.

"Together."

Wind brushed across the bridge again, carrying away the last of the morning fog.

For the first time in both their lives, they felt the boundary of the world shift—not tearing, not breaking, but bending, making space for something that had been waiting for centuries.

They remained on the bridge until the light changed.

Not speaking.

Not touching.

Just breathing—side by side—
as if relearning the rhythm of a connection older than memory.

Chapter 8 : The Unfinished Panel

The Louvre's private archives were not part of any tour, public or private. They existed below the museum like a quiet undercurrent—rooms of controlled darkness, steel racks, sealed drawers, and paintings that never made it to the walls upstairs.

Leon had hesitated before suggesting they go there.

It wasn't forbidden for him to enter. But bringing someone with him—someone outside conservation—was not strictly allowed.

Yet something about this connection, this shared thread pulling them both toward an unnamed place, made him cross boundaries he once respected absolutely.

After leaving the Pont des Arts, they walked in silence toward the museum, slipping into the staff entrance behind a group of restorers carrying boxed materials. No one questioned them. Leon's badge opened the inner door, and Mina followed close behind, her steps slow but certain.

She didn't ask where they were going.
She didn't need to.

Her intuition mirrored his.

They went down two levels—past staff corridors, past temperature-controlled storerooms, past the old freight elevator whose metal cage doors rattled like a relic from another era.

Finally, they reached a corridor lined with metal cabinets and storage racks. The air grew cooler, the lighting dimmer. Their footsteps echoed softly in the narrow hallway.

Leon stopped at a heavy gray door marked with a numerical code.

Before he typed it in, he looked at Mina.

"You don't have to go inside," he said quietly.

She held his gaze. "I do."

He nodded once and entered the code.
The lock clicked open.
The door swung inward.

Inside was a long room lit by overhead fixtures that hummed faintly. Paintings—some framed, some raw, some mounted, some still on stretchers—rested on sliding racks that moved like the pages of a massive metal book.

Leon guided her past several racks, letting them pass landscapes, religious scenes, studies of hands, unfinished portraits.

He stopped near the end of the room.

"This one," he said softly.

He pulled the rack toward them with a slow, steady force.

The metal made a low rumbling sound as the rack slid outward.

An unfinished Renaissance panel appeared, its wood darkened by centuries but its paint still partly intact. The panel was narrower than the Mona Lisa, smaller, more intimate. No frame, no protective glass—just raw wood, the grain visible at the edges.

Mina stepped closer.

Her breath hitched.

The portrait on the panel was incomplete—
but impossible to mistake.

A woman's face lightly sketched in charcoal, the beginnings of a smile emerging in faint strokes, the eyes half-painted, as if the artist had begun them with great care but stopped before they could be fully realized.

The left eye was more defined than the right.
The hands were only shadows.
The dress was blocked in with broad strokes.
The background was a vague wash of earthy tones.

Yet despite its incompletion, the portrait radiated presence.

Mina felt a tremor along her spine.

Her hand rose slowly, almost involuntarily, stopping a few centimeters from the wood.

She whispered:

"I know this."

Leon turned sharply to her.

"What do you mean?"

She shook her head, her breath unsteady.

"I don't know. But I've seen this. Not here. Not in any museum. Before."

He watched her closely, the tension in his shoulders tightening.

She stepped closer, eyes fixed on the panel.

"The way the head tilts," she whispered. "The way the eyes look slightly to the left. The way the lips are shaped but not yet complete..."

Her voice faltered.

Leon spoke quietly, almost reluctantly.

"This panel... wasn't supposed to be seen by anyone outside the archive."

"Why not?"

"Because it's anonymous," he said. "Its origin is disputed. It appeared in the museum's collections after the war. No record of the artist. No signature. No documentation. Just... the work itself."

Mina swallowed.

"Why did you bring me to see it?"

Leon hesitated.

Then he reached into the inner pocket of his coat and pulled out a folded piece of paper.

He handed it to her.

She unfolded it.

Her eyes widened.

It was the sketch he had drawn the night before—the rough portrait, the loose lines, the impression of her face.

Except—

The shape of the jaw.
The tilt of the head.
The half-formed smile.
They mirrored the unfinished panel with eerie accuracy.

Mina's knees nearly weakened.

"This…" She looked between the sketch and the panel, her pulse racing. "You didn't know about this painting?"

"I've seen it," he said. "Years ago. Once. But I didn't think of it yesterday. Not consciously."

She looked sharply at him. "But you drew…"

"I drew what came to mind," he said. "What I saw."

"Saw where?"

He didn't answer.

She stepped closer to the panel, her breath warm against the cool air.

"This face," she whispered, "I feel like I've held this expression before. Like I've tried to smile this way. Not in a mirror. But… sitting somewhere. For someone."

Leon's eyes darkened with understanding.

"And the painter?" he asked softly.

She closed her eyes.

In the darkness behind her eyelids, the studio appeared again—
the light falling across her lap,
the painter looking up in concentration,
the unfinished smile she felt on her own lips.

She opened her eyes.

Her voice was barely audible.

"He felt... familiar."

Silence filled the room—thick, electric, undeniable.

Leon took a slow breath.

"This panel," he said quietly, "has been examined by multiple experts. Some believe it might be a discarded study by an apprentice. Others think it could be a copy of a lost work. No one agrees. No one knows."

He paused.

"And yet, when I look at it... it feels unfinished. Not because the artist abandoned it, but because something interrupted it."

Mina's pulse quickened.

"What do you mean?"

Leon's gaze deepened, his voice low.

"As if the painting was meant to become something... but the moment it was supposed to capture was broken."

A shiver ran through her bloodstream.

"Do you think this..." She gestured to the panel, the sketch, the air between them. "Do you think this is connected to... us?"

He didn't look away.

"Yes," he said.

The word settled like a weight in her chest—heavy, frightening, but not unwelcome.

She stepped back from the panel, suddenly aware of how loud her heartbeat had become in the quiet archive room.

Leon watched her, his posture gentle but tense, as if he feared saying too much too quickly.

She lifted a trembling hand to her forehead.

"This isn't possible," she murmured.

"Neither is sharing the same dream," he said softly.

Her breath caught.

He stepped closer—not touching, not reaching, but standing near enough that his presence steadied her.

"Mina," he said quietly, "we are not imagining this."

Her eyes met his.

There was no fear in them now—
only recognition and the beginning of truth.

"What do we do?" she whispered.

Leon exhaled slowly.

"We find out who we were," he said.

"And why we're here now."

She nodded once—small, frightened, but resolute.

He gently slid the rack closed, the unfinished panel disappearing into the dimness.

As the metal door rumbled shut, Mina felt a strange sensation in her chest.

A pull backward, into something ancient.
And a pull forward, into something inevitable.

For a brief second, she wondered which direction her life now belonged to.

Then the lock clicked into place.

And the sound echoed through her like a memory returning home.

Chapter 9: The Name in the Margins

For the rest of the afternoon, the world outside the Louvre seemed almost unreal to both of them. The crowds, the sound of footsteps, the rustling of coats, the sharp winter air—all of it felt like a thin veil stretched over another reality they had stepped into without warning.

Leon and Mina left the archives in silence, not because there was nothing to say, but because there was too much.

He led her through the staff corridors until they reached a research room he often used—a narrow space with high shelves, soft yellow lamps, and long tables pushed together like an academic workshop frozen in time.

It was empty at this hour.

Leon locked the door from the inside.

Mina glanced around. "What is this room?"

"Documentation," he said. "Records of provenance, restoration notes, acquisition logs, historical studies. Most of it is digitized now, but older files remain only on paper."

"And you think we might find something here?"

Leon hesitated for the briefest moment.

Then he said quietly, "I think we already have."

He walked to a drawer labeled 16th Century: Italian Panels — Unattributed and pulled it open. Inside were folders bound with string, their edges frayed from decades of use.

He removed one and set it on the table.

It belonged to the unfinished panel they had just seen.

He untied the string and opened the folder. Mina stood beside him, leaning slightly forward to see.

Inside were notes written by various curators and restorers over the years—some typed, some handwritten, some yellowed and brittle. There were sketches, cross-sections of paint layers, wood analyses, and a few old black-and-white photographs.

But what drew Leon's eyes wasn't the technical data.

It was a folded page tucked between two rigid sheets of archival paper.

He lifted it carefully.

Mina felt her breath still.

The paper was older than the rest, darker, with edges that had begun to crumble. The handwriting on it was elegant, slanted, unmistakably Renaissance—ink faded, but readable.

"What is this?" she whispered.

"It's not catalogued," Leon said. "I've never seen it in the file before."

He smoothed the page gently.

As the creases flattened, one line stood out:

"...ritratto della donna che chiamava Mina..."
"...portrait of the woman he called Mina..."

Mina felt the air leave her lungs.

She pressed her fingertips against the edge of the table to steady herself.

"Leon..." Her voice cracked. "That's my name."

He nodded slowly, eyes never leaving the page.

"This isn't a name anyone in Renaissance Italy would casually write," he said. "It wasn't common. It wasn't... ordinary."

She felt something rise in her—a tremor of disbelief mixed with a deeper, heavier recognition.

"Is there more?" she asked, barely able to speak.

Leon read aloud, translating softly from Italian:

"The unfinished work remains here.
The painter has fallen ill,
and though he began with great intent,
he says he cannot complete her,
for her expression eludes him.
He says she smiles for no one.
Except him.
The woman, Mina, visits still,
but sits no longer.
There is something between them
that is not for paint to capture."

The room seemed to tilt.

Mina closed her eyes, her breath shivering outward. The words felt like hands reaching through centuries, touching something buried at the base of her spine.

Leon continued, voice barely audible:

"He calls her his unfinished truth.
And she calls him..."

Leon stopped.

Mina opened her eyes.

"What?" she whispered. "What did she call him?"

Leon swallowed once, staring at the faded line.

"...Lione."
Lion.
Leon.

The room fell completely silent.

Mina stepped backward as if struck, her hand lifting instinctively to her mouth.

"That's..."

Her voice failed.

Leon didn't move.

He didn't need to.

Everything inside him had already shifted.

"This can't be real," Mina said, but even as the words escaped her, certainty hollowed her chest.

Leon looked up at her slowly, and for the first time since they met, there was fear in his eyes—not of her, not of the past, but of the truth they were unearthing together.

"Mina," he said quietly, "this document is from the 1500s."

Her pulse hammered violently.

"And your name," he continued, "is written in it."

The word *your* didn't refer to the present.

It referred to something older, deeper, something that wound through the dream they both saw, through the unfinished panel, through the way they recognized each other long before they exchanged names.

Mina pressed her palms against the table, leaning forward as though afraid her legs would give out.

"Read the rest," she breathed.

Leon nodded and lowered his eyes to the page.

"She sits beside him as he rests,
always in quiet. They speak little,
for their words are unnecessary.
I believe the painter loves her,
but not as men usually love women.
It is something rarer,
something I cannot name."

Mina's shoulders shook.

Leon read the final line.

"He says he knew her before he painted her.
And fears he will know her again."

A tremor passed through Mina's entire body.

Leon set the document down slowly, reverently, as though placing a fragile truth onto the table.

Neither of them spoke for several seconds.

Finally, Mina whispered:

"So it wasn't just dreams."

Leon shook his head.

"No," he said softly. "It wasn't."

Her voice was trembling now.

"What does this mean for us?"

Leon stepped closer, not touching her but standing near enough that she felt the warmth of his presence.

"It means," he said gently, "that whatever connection we have… didn't begin here."

She lifted her eyes to his—filled with fear, wonder, and an emerging certainty that felt older than her own breath.

Leon continued, his voice low, steady:

"Mina, I think we knew each other before we were born."

Her throat tightened.

"And now," he whispered, "we've found each other again."

The words seemed to settle in the air between them, neither frightening nor unbelievable—only true.

Mina felt tears prick behind her eyes, not from sadness but from an overwhelming, impossible recognition that reached beyond time.

She closed the distance between them by one small step.

"Leon," she said softly, "what do we do with this?"

He looked at her with an ache in his expression that felt centuries deep.

"We follow it," he said.
"Wherever it leads."

She nodded once—small, decisive.

And in that moment, the centuries folded quietly, like pages aligning.

Chapter 10: The Studio Returns

Leon locked the archive door behind them, but the sound of the lock felt distant—muted beneath the weight of what they had just read. Mina stood still in the corridor, her breath uneven, her eyes fixed somewhere far beyond the fluorescent-lit walls.

The hallway felt too modern, too narrow, too present.

She turned to Leon.

"Can we go somewhere quieter?" she asked.

He nodded. There was no hesitation. He led her up a short flight of stairs to a small, unused viewing room—once meant for staff presentations, now empty except for a table, two chairs, and a large window that looked out onto a service courtyard. The light inside was soft, muted by dust on the overhead lamps.

He closed the door.

Mina walked to the window and pressed her hand lightly against the cold glass. Her shoulders rose and fell rapidly, as if her own breath were too loud in her ears.

Leon remained near the door, watching her, waiting—not wanting to push, not wanting to speak before she was ready.

She finally turned.

"I need to understand," she said. "All of it. But every time I try to think clearly, something else... interrupts."

Leon stepped closer—not touching her, just enough to let her feel he was there.

"What interrupts?" he asked softly.

She tried to find the words.

"It's like I'm carrying two sets of memories," she said, her voice trembling. "Mine... and something else. Something that doesn't belong to this life."

Leon's breath tightened.

"Mina—"

But she lifted a hand, stopping him.

"I'm afraid," she said quietly. "Not of you. Not even of what we found. I'm afraid because parts of me… recognize this too easily."

He nodded. "I feel the same."

She swallowed hard. "Every time I look at the unfinished panel, I feel… pulled. As if some part of me is trying to return somewhere I've already been."

Leon exhaled shakily.

"That's why I wanted to bring you here," he said. "There's something I haven't shown anyone. Something I didn't understand until now."

He walked to the small table and opened the leather portfolio he had brought earlier. He hesitated, his fingers lingering on the edge of the paper inside.

Then he pulled out a single sheet and placed it on the table.

"Yesterday," he said quietly, "after I went home… I drew again."

Mina stepped closer.

The sketch was not rough this time. It was detailed, precise, more deliberate than anything he had shown her.

A woman in Renaissance dress.
Hands folded.
Head tilted slightly to the left.
Eyes soft, half-focused—
not at the painter, not at the viewer, but at someone behind the moment.

Mina's breath hitched.

"It's the same gesture," she whispered, her voice breaking. "The same… as the panel."

He nodded.

"I didn't intend to draw her," he said. "I was thinking of you."

The words settled heavily in the room.

She looked at the sketch again.

And then something inside her shifted.

Her vision blurred—not from tears, though they pricked behind her eyes—but from a sudden, sharp brightness in the air around her.

She stepped back reflexively.

"Mina?" Leon moved toward her, alarmed. "Are you—"

Her hand reached blindly for the table.

"I'm dizzy," she whispered. "No... not dizzy. It's something else."

Leon took her elbow gently to steady her.

The room blurred—
not fading, but shifting, like two transparencies sliding over each other.

The table remained.
The window remained.
Leon's hand on her arm remained.

But something else—
something from centuries ago—
pressed against the modern room with unmistakable force.

A beam of light moved across the floor.
Not from the small window.
From a tall, narrow window with shutters—
a window that did not exist.

The air grew warmer.
Dust spun in a sunlit column.
The faint scent of linseed oil drifted in.

Leon felt it too.

His breath stopped.

"Mina..." he whispered.

She lifted her head.

The viewing room fractured.

On one side:
the present—dusty lamps, white walls, glass windows.

On the other side:
the studio—wooden beams, rough floors, the painter's tools laid out neatly on a workbench.

Two realities overlapped.

Not in a dream.

Not in memory.

Here.
Now.
With both of them awake.

Mina's fingers tightened on Leon's sleeve.

The wooden chair from the dream appeared—
not fully, but as a faint outline pressing through the light.

Leon felt the hairs rise along his arms.

He saw an easel—
an old one, with carved edges, holding a wooden panel that was only half-painted.

He stepped back, instinctively shielding Mina.

The past pulsed once—
a deep, silent heartbeat.

Then the overlapping image sharpened—
as if someone behind time had turned the focus ring of a lens.

The painter appeared.

Not fully formed, not solid, but neither ghostly nor imagined. A presence. A figure emerging from within the merged realities.

Leon couldn't breathe.

Mina pressed a hand to her chest, her pulse erratic.

The painter turned his head—
and though his features were softened by the layers of time, his eyes were clear.

Deep.
Knowing.
Warm.

He looked directly at Mina first.

A faint, unmistakable recognition lit his expression.

Then he looked at Leon.

Not with confusion.
Not with fear.

With the quiet acceptance of someone who understood the shape of destiny better than those living inside it.

Mina's breath came out in a sharp tremor.

"Leon..." she whispered, barely able to form the words. "Do you see him?"

Leon's voice broke.

"Yes."

The painter lifted a hand slightly—
not in greeting,
but in acknowledgement.

The room vibrated softly, like a thin veil torn at the edges.

Mina felt her knees weaken.
Leon steadied her.

And then—

The studio flickered.

The painter's outline wavered.

A flash of sunlight across the wooden floor.
A faint echo of a woman's laughter—
soft, distant, familiar.

Then everything collapsed inward—

Light.
Color.
Sound.
Time.

Both realities folded back into one.

The studio vanished.
The viewing room returned.
Dust settled in the air.

Mina gasped and clutched Leon's shirt for balance.

He pulled her close in pure instinct—
steadying her as she trembled.

They stood like that for several seconds, breathing the same uneven breath, their
hearts still echoing the impossible.

Mina pulled back slightly, her eyes wide, luminous with shock.

"That was real," she whispered.

Leon's voice was hoarse.

"Yes."

She touched her temple, dazed.

"He looked at us," she said. "Not at the air. Not at the past. At us."

Leon nodded.

"And he recognized us," he said quietly. "Both of us."

Mina's hands trembled violently.

"Leon…"
Her eyes filled with tears.
"What is happening to us?"

He didn't have an answer.

He only knew the world they thought they lived in had just cracked open—and something ancient, unfinished, and deeply theirs had stepped through.

He took her trembling hands gently in his own.

"Mina," he said softly, "whatever this is… we're not imagining it."

For the first time, she didn't deny it.

She nodded.

Tears slipped down her cheek—
not from fear,
but from recognition so profound it hurt.

Leon wiped them gently with the back of his knuckle.

Their foreheads almost touched.

Both felt the trembling boundary between past and present quivering again.

Not breaking.

Just waiting.

Chapter 11: The Letter Hidden in the Frame

They did not leave the room for a long time.

Not because they were afraid—
but because the world outside no longer felt entirely separate from the one they had just touched.

Mina sat slowly, hands still trembling slightly. Leon remained standing for a moment, watching her with an intensity he couldn't disguise. The fragile calm between them felt like the thin surface of water after something enormous had just passed beneath.

"Leon," Mina said softly, "we saw the same thing."

"Yes."

"And he saw us."

His jaw tightened. "Yes."

She looked up at him, eyes still wide from the shock.
"I'm not losing my mind."

"No," he said, kneeling beside her, "you're not."

Their foreheads nearly touched again—
not as lovers,
but as two people bracing themselves inside a truth larger than either of them.

When she finally steadied, she spoke again.

"You said there was something else," she whispered. "Something you never showed anyone."

Leon hesitated.

Then he rose to his feet, inhaled slowly, and offered her his hand.

"Come with me."

Mina took it.

He led her back down the stairs, through another corridor, deeper into the archive storage. They moved quickly now, driven by an unspoken urgency.

When they reached the heavy door to the unfinished panel, Leon paused.

He typed the code.
The lock clicked.
The door opened.

They stepped inside.

The air was colder than before, as though the room itself sensed something shifting. Leon pulled the rack toward them again. The unfinished panel emerged from the darkness.

They stood before it in silence.

The faint charcoal lines of the woman's face—her face—looked back at them with that half-begun serenity, the smile not yet formed, the eyes waiting for something they had never received.

Mina swallowed hard.

"Why does this feel like…"

"Like walking into a memory?" Leon finished for her.

She nodded.

He exhaled.
"Mina… there is a part of this I've never told anyone."

He reached into the inner pocket of his coat and pulled out a small, thin tool—one used for examining cracks in paint and the edges of wooden panels.

He stepped closer to the painting.

Mina's breath caught.
"Leon—"

"I'm not harming it," he assured her gently. "Just… showing you something I found years ago."

He lifted the panel slightly, revealing the back—simple wood, aged, dark, with a faint seam running along one edge.

He touched the seam.

Mina frowned. "What is that?"

"It's not part of the panel," he said. "It's a compartment."

Her pulse quickened. "How do you know?"

"Because I opened it once," he said quietly. "I shouldn't have. But I did."

She stared at him.

"And what was inside?"

Leon didn't answer.
He simply pressed gently along the seam.
The wood shifted with a soft, reluctant creak.

A hidden sliver of space opened.

Mina inhaled sharply.

Inside was a thin, folded scrap of parchment—fragile with age, edges curled. Leon reached in carefully and removed it.

He didn't open it yet.

Mina's voice was barely a whisper.

"You kept this secret?"

"Yes."

"Why?"

"Because I didn't understand it," he said. "And I didn't want anyone else to mistake it for forgery, or coincidence, or madness."

He met her eyes.

"Until now."

He unfolded the parchment with meticulous care.

Time had yellowed it deeply. The ink had faded, but the writing remained visible— thin, elegant strokes in Italian from half a millennium ago.

Mina instinctively reached for Leon's hand.

He let her hold it.

He began to read.

"A chi troverà questo,
to the one who finds this,
io scrivo con un cuore che già sa ciò che il tempo nasconderà,
I write with a heart that already knows what time will hide,
che lei tornerà.
that she will return.
Ma non nello stesso secolo,
But not in the same century,
non nello stesso corpo,
not in the same body,
ma con lo stesso sguardo.
but with the same gaze.
E quando tornerà,
And when she returns,
non dipingerò il suo volto,
I will not paint her face,
ma sarà lei a riconoscere il mio.
but she will be the one to recognize mine.
E allora,
And then,
capirò che non era un quadro incompiuto,
I will understand that it was not an unfinished painting,
ma un amore incompiuto.
but an unfinished love."

Mina's knees weakened.

Leon caught her instinctively.

She pressed her forehead against his chest, her breath breaking.

"Leon..." Her voice faltered. "He was writing to... me."

Leon's throat tightened.
He placed a shaking hand over her back.

"He didn't know your future name," Leon whispered, voice ragged. "But he knew you."

Mina closed her eyes. Tears slid down her cheeks without resistance.

Leon continued reading, voice trembling now.

"*Se lei vedrà questo,*
If she sees this,
significa che non abbiamo finito.
it means we were not finished.
E se lei sarà con qualcuno...
And if she is with someone..."

Leon stopped suddenly.

He stared at the next words, hands trembling.

Mina looked up. "What does it say?"

Leon swallowed hard.

"*...allora sarà colui che è stato me.*
then she will be with the one who was me."

Silence rang in the room.

Mina stepped back slowly, tears still falling, her hand over her mouth.
"Leon..." Her voice broke. "He knew you. He knew you would... return."

Leon felt the world tilt beneath him—
not frighteningly,
but as if the ground had shifted to reveal something truer underneath.

He read the final line aloud.

*"E finalmente
ci ritroveremo.
And finally,
we will find each other again."*

The parchment trembled in his hands.

Mina pressed a hand to her heart, sobbing once—a quiet, broken sound pulled from a depth she didn't know existed.

Leon reached out and wiped the tears from her face, his touch gentle, reverent.

"Mina," he whispered, "this wasn't a coincidence."

She shook her head, breath trembling.

"It's... us," she said. "It was always us."

He stepped toward her.

And this time, she didn't step back.

Their foreheads touched, breaths mingling.

Two lives.
Two centuries.
One unfinished love returning through time.

The moment hung in the air between them—
fragile, ancient, and achingly real.

And neither of them could deny it anymore.

Chapter 12: The Day the Smile Begins

They left the archive room in silence, carrying the parchment in a protective sleeve as if it were a heartbeat made fragile by time. The hallway felt narrower than before—as if the walls themselves sensed something between them had shifted and were quietly closing in to witness it.

Leon locked the door behind them with slow, deliberate motions.
Mina stood beside him, her breathing still shallow, her palm pressed lightly to her sternum, as though trying to steady the thrum beneath her ribs.

She felt his presence at her side—
not touching,
not crowding,
but anchoring her in the only way he could.

"Let's go upstairs," he said softly.

She nodded.

They climbed the stairs together, neither rushing nor lingering, simply moving through the museum as if through a dream—an old dream made real.

The upper floor was nearly empty that afternoon. Only a few tourists walked the main hall, speaking in hushed tones. Leon led her to a quieter gallery, one with a long wooden bench in the center and tall windows that diffused the cold Paris light into something soft and pearlescent.

Mina sat.

Leon sat beside her.

They didn't speak at first. They needed the silence—
not to hide in,
but to let their minds adjust to the truth that had just unfolded.

Finally she turned to him.

"I keep thinking," she said, her voice barely above a whisper, "about the line he wrote. 'Un amore incompiuto'... an unfinished love."

Leon's jaw tightened slightly. "Yes."

"It feels..." She hesitated, searching for words that didn't yet exist. "It feels like something inside me has been waiting for that sentence. Waiting for centuries."

Leon didn't interrupt.

She looked down at her hands, fingers trembling. "When I read it, I felt something break open in me. Something I didn't know I was missing."

Leon's chest tightened.

She lifted her gaze. "Do you feel it too?"

He nodded.

"Where?" she asked softly.

He placed two fingers against his sternum. "Here."

Her breath caught.

"Leon," she whispered, "why can I remember the light in that studio? Why can I remember the smell of the oil, the way the dress felt, the way he looked at me? Why does it feel more real than parts of my own childhood?"

He inhaled slowly.

"Memories can hide," he said. "They can sleep for lifetimes."

Mina closed her eyes. "So when I dream..."

"You're not dreaming," he said. "You're remembering."

She opened her eyes.

And something in her gaze changed.
Softened.
Deepened.
Recovered.

A faint tremor moved through her body.

"Leon," she said, "I think... I think I remember the smile."

He frowned gently. "What smile?"

She swallowed.

"The one he painted. The one he tried to paint. The one he said was for him alone."

Leon felt his pulse spike.

She pressed both hands to her face, covering her eyes as if ashamed of what she was about to confess.

"I remember sitting in that chair," she whispered. "I remember him telling me not to smile too much, because he couldn't capture it right. And I remember..."

Her voice shook.

Leon leaned closer, listening with every part of himself.

"I remember wanting to smile for him anyway."

Her hands fell away from her face. Tears clung to her lashes, making her eyes luminous and overwhelming.

Leon inhaled sharply—
not because of her tears,
but because he remembered something too.

A fragment.
A flash.
Not from a dream.
Not from the sketch.
From somewhere deeper.

He saw her—
the woman in the chair—
tilting her head slightly, almost shyly.
The beginnings of a smile touching her mouth, delicate, trembling, incomplete.

He saw himself—
in another lifetime—
lowering his brush, breath catching, not because he couldn't paint it
but because he couldn't bear the intimacy of what he saw.

He blinked hard.

Mina saw the shift in him and straightened, her breath catching.

"You remember," she whispered.

"I... saw something."
His voice was rough.
"A moment. A smile that wasn't finished."

Her lips parted.

"And you," he added, "were looking at me the same way you looked at the unfinished panel."

Mina pressed a hand to her mouth, stifling a sob so sharp it seemed pulled from the deepest part of her being.

She rose suddenly from the bench, pacing a few steps away, trying to breathe, trying to make sense of a reality that had split open and was rearranging itself inside her.

Leon watched her.

She turned back to him, her voice breaking:

"Why do I feel like I've been mourning you my whole life without knowing why?"

Leon stood slowly.

The quiet between them became charged.

He approached her, each step careful, deliberate.

When he reached her, he stopped just close enough that she could feel the warmth of him, but not close enough to touch.

He lifted a hand—slowly, so she could retreat if she needed to.

She didn't.

He brushed a tear from her cheek.

Her breath hitched.

"Because," he said softly, his voice deep and trembling, "we were separated before we finished."

Her knees weakened.

He caught her by the elbows, steadying her gently.

She clung to him—not out of passion, not out of desire, but out of a recognition so ancient it scraped against the core of her being.

He held her.

They stayed like that—
two people who had loved each other in another life and had been forced apart before they could understand what they were.

Mina whispered into his shoulder:

"I'm remembering more."

Leon closed his eyes.

"What do you see?"

She pulled back slightly, her eyes unfocused as if glimpsing something over his shoulder.

"The studio," she whispered. "But... not the part where I'm sitting. Another part. A moment after."

"What moment?"

She swallowed hard.

"When he—when you—"

Her voice thinned.
"When you told me why the smile was unfinished."

Leon's heart pounded painfully.

"Mina," he whispered, "what did I say?"

She met his eyes.

"You said," she breathed, "'I cannot finish the smile because I don't know how our story ends.'"

Leon's breath fractured.

"And now?" he whispered.

Her voice trembled.

"Now we know the story didn't end."

They stood facing each other, breaths shallow, hearts shaking, time folding quietly around them.

Mina's gaze softened, the faintest hint of the beginning of a smile touching her lips.

Not the smile from the painting.
Not yet.
But the smile from the memory.

And for the first time in this lifetime, Leon felt the echo of it.

The echo of a love that had waited centuries not to begin—
but to continue.

Chapter 13: The Painter's Last Day

The winter evening settled over Paris like a veil, soft and pale, carrying a quiet that did not belong to the modern world. Leon and Mina left the museum together, but they did not speak. They walked through the courtyard beneath the arcades, under the last wash of daylight, each lost in a part of memory that had begun to return.

They crossed the Pont Royal, the iron railing cold beneath their hands. The Seine flowed below them, dark, reflective, as if carrying the weight of centuries.

Halfway across the bridge, Mina stopped.

Her breath hitched.

Leon immediately turned.
"What is it?"

She took a step back from the railing, eyes wide, hands trembling.

"It's happening again," she whispered.

He stepped to her side, ready to catch her if she swayed.

"What do you see?"

She stared past him—not at the Paris skyline, not at the present—but into a distance where time seemed to fold like soft cloth.

Her voice came out in pieces.

"I see... the end."

Leon's chest tightened.

"What end?"

Mina swallowed, her pupils dilating slightly, as though her mind were slipping into a space that belonged to someone older, someone who had died long before she was born.

"The day everything stopped," she whispered. "The day the smile became unfinished."

Leon's hand hovered near her waist, not touching, but ready to hold her steady.

"How far back are you?" he asked softly.

Her breath trembled.

"Five hundred years."

The world around her dimmed, but she didn't faint. She remained standing on the bridge—but the Paris evening began to dissolve around her like falling ash.

Light reshaped itself.

Colors shifted.

Stone turned to wood.

The Seine's sound faded, replaced by the quiet murmur of a distant countryside stream.

She gasped—once, sharply—as she found herself standing inside the Renaissance studio.

Not a vision.
Not a dream.
A memory returning in its full, crushing clarity.

She clutched the railing of the bridge in the present, but her mind gripped the wooden edge of the old workbench.

Leon's voice reached her, distant but anchoring.

"I'm right here," he murmured. "Tell me what you see."

She nodded faintly, eyes unfocused.

"It's the last day," she whispered. "You... he... was painting. But he wasn't well."

A tremor moved through her voice.

"He was coughing. A lot. He tried to hide it, but I knew."

"What else?" Leon asked softly.

She inhaled shakily.

"The light was different," she murmured. "It wasn't morning. It was late afternoon. The shadows were long, and the room was colder than usual. He was wearing a thicker coat. He kept warming his hands near the candle."

Leon closed his eyes.

The painter.
The illness.
The waning light.
It matched the fragment of history that had always seemed unclear.

"He told me to sit," Mina continued, her breath trembling. "But his voice…" She touched her throat. "His voice was weak. He couldn't finish the sentence without coughing."

Leon's fingers curled against the railing, knuckles white.

"I sat anyway," she whispered. "Not for the painting. For him."

A tear slid down her cheek.

"He looked at me the way you look at me now—like he was afraid time was running out."

Leon felt a sharp pain in his chest.

"What happened next?" he asked.

Mina blinked slowly, tears spilling freely now.

"He started the smile again," she said. "He lifted the brush… but his hand shook. He tried to steady it against the wood. He tried so hard. But he couldn't capture it. Not this time."

Her voice broke.

"He looked frustrated. Not with me. With himself. With time. With his body failing."

Leon swallowed hard.

"And then…"

Her breath hitched.

"He dropped the brush."

A small, pained sound escaped her throat.

"He tried to pick it up. He tried to apologize. I remember grabbing his hand to stop him. I told him he didn't have to finish it."

Leon felt his heart fracture.

"What did I say?" he asked.

Mina closed her eyes.

Her voice became soft, trembling.

"You said… 'I'm not afraid of dying. I'm afraid of leaving you unfinished.'"

Leon's breath broke.

He reached for her hand—this time, actually holding it.

She clung to him.

"And then," she continued, "you leaned back in the chair. You were too weak to stand. I knelt beside you. I held your hands. You smiled… barely. And you said—"

She sobbed once, the sound sharp and painful.

"'Promise me you will find me again.'"

Leon felt tears sting his own eyes.

"And I said," Mina whispered, "'I will find you in any century.'"

The bridge around them was silent.

Paris was still.

Only their breaths moved between them.

"And then…" Mina's voice broke completely. "You closed your eyes. And I kept holding your hands until they weren't warm anymore."

Leon couldn't breathe.

He pulled her into his arms—without hesitation, without question—holding her the way he must have held her then.

Her head pressed under his chin.

Her tears soaked into his coat.

And his own tears fell into her hair—silent, unstoppable.

The past and present merged inside that embrace.
Two lifetimes folding into each other.

She whispered into his chest:

"That's why the smile was unfinished."

He held her tighter.

"And that's why we're here now."

They remained like that—two souls who had been torn apart by time and stitched back together by memory.

Neither spoke for a long time.

Finally, Mina lifted her head slightly.

Her lashes were wet.
Her mouth trembled.

Her eyes shone not with fear but with recognition.

"We didn't get to finish anything," she whispered. "Not the painting. Not the love. Not the life."

Leon cupped her face gently.

"And now," he murmured, "we have another chance."

She closed her eyes, letting his thumbs wipe her tears away.

Her voice trembled softly.

"I'm not afraid anymore."

He lowered his forehead to hers.

"Neither am I."

The river flowed beneath them.

Time—past and present—flowed inside them.

And somewhere between the two, the smile that was once left unfinished
began
to return.

Chapter 14: The First Night of the New Life

They walked back from the bridge slowly, not because their steps were heavy, but because the air between them had changed. The world no longer felt like a simple, linear place. Paris seemed to hum with a deeper resonance, as though every street, every stone beneath their feet recognized what had happened on the Pont Royal.

Leon didn't let go of her hand.
Mina didn't try to pull hers away.

Their fingers intertwined naturally—
not rushed,
not trembling,
simply right.

It was nothing like the way lovers in the present century chose each other.
It was quieter.
Older.
Certain.

As they reached the quieter streets near Saint-Germain, Mina finally broke the silence.

"I don't know how to live after remembering something like that," she said softly.

Leon looked at her—really looked at her—with a warmth that was both new and ancient.

"We live slowly," he said. "We breathe. We let the world be simple for one night."

She exhaled—a shaky breath she hadn't realized she'd been holding.

"One night," she repeated. "Just one."

He nodded.

But the meaning between them was clear:
one night to begin the new life,
not to escape the old one.

They found a small restaurant tucked between a bookstore and a flower shop. Warm light spilled from the windows, casting a gold haze on the sidewalk. The scent of baked bread and simmering herbs drifted out whenever the door opened.

Leon held it for her.

Inside, the place was nearly empty—an elderly couple at one table, a man reading alone at another, the soft sound of plates being stacked in the kitchen.

Mina slid into a small wooden booth.
Leon sat across from her.

The waiter brought water.
Menus.
A candle was lit between them.

It burned softly, steady.

Mina stared at the flame, then at Leon, feeling the weight in her chest shift—not painful, not overwhelming, but tender.

"It's strange," she murmured. "I feel like I've known you forever. And also like I'm just now meeting you properly."

Leon gave a faint, warm smile.

"I think both are true."

She lowered her gaze.
"Are you afraid?"

He reached across the table and gently touched her wrist.

"Only of one thing."

She looked up sharply.

"What?"

"Rushing this," he said. "Rushing us. After centuries apart, I don't want to lose a single moment."

Her breath softened.

The waiter returned. They ordered simple dishes—he chose roasted chicken with thyme, she ordered a vegetable soup. Two glasses of red wine. They ate slowly, quietly, relishing the warmth, the normalcy, the soft clatter of cutlery.

Halfway through the meal, Mina set her spoon down.

"Leon?" Her voice was quiet, unsure.

He looked up. "Yes?"

"When I remembered today… I felt something terrible."

He leaned in, attentive.

"Not just sadness," she whispered. "A fear that if we finally found each other again… something might take it away again."

Leon's chest tightened painfully.

"I won't let anything take you," he said.

She shook her head gently.
"It's not something you can control. Time… fate… life."

He reached out, covered her hand with both of his.

"Mina. Listen to me."
His voice deepened. "We lost each other once. But today proved something."

"What?"

"That even death can't keep us apart."

Her heart thudded once—hard.

He continued, softer:

"We are not bound by one lifetime. Or one story. We're bound by something deeper. Something that waited patiently for centuries for the moment we could continue."

Mina looked down at their hands—his fingers strong but gentle, her fingers small, trembling but warm.

She intertwined them deliberately.

"Then let's continue slowly," she whispered. "No fear. No rushing. Just… us."

Leon nodded.

"Us," he echoed.

A quiet assurance settled between them.

After dinner, they stepped back into the night. Paris glowed softly—street lamps casting long halos in the mist, a violinist playing near a corner, the distant hum of cars fading into the deepening evening.

They walked side by side, not speaking, letting the city be their witness.

When they reached the intersection where their paths diverged—
her apartment to the left,
his to the right—
they stopped.

Mina looked up at him.

Leon waited, giving her space.

She took a breath, then spoke:

"I don't want to be alone tonight."

Leon felt something inside him stutter—not desire, not impulse, but recognition.

"Then come with me," he said quietly. "Not to rush anything. Not to cross any boundaries. Just to rest. To breathe. To be together without the weight of centuries crushing us."

Her eyes softened.

She nodded.

His apartment was small, minimalist, filled with books and sketches and warm shadows. Mina stepped inside, inhaling the faint scent of charcoal and old paper.

Leon removed his coat and hung hers gently beside it, as though the simple gesture meant more than he could say aloud.

"Tea?" he offered.

She nodded.

He moved to the small kitchen. She watched him quietly. There was something grounding about the ordinary movements—the way he filled the kettle, the way he set out two ceramic cups, the way he paused when he sensed her watching him.

He returned with two steaming mugs and set them on the coffee table.

Mina sat on the couch.

Leon sat beside her—close, but not touching.

They sipped in silence.

Finally she rested her head against his shoulder, slowly, tentatively, as though afraid he might pull away.

He didn't.

He shifted slightly, just enough to support her weight comfortably.

Mina closed her eyes.
Her breath steadied.
Leon felt her relax—really relax—for the first time since they met.

After several minutes, she spoke.

"Leon... can I ask something?"

"Anything."

"If we met in another life... why do you think we found each other now?"

He took a long, slow breath.

"Because," he said, "this time, nothing stopped us."

Mina's fingers curled gently into the fabric of his sleeve.

"And because," he added, voice deepening, "this time, we're free to finish what was left unfinished."

She nodded against him.

A soft warmth spread through her chest.

Not passion.
Not desire.
Something deeper.

He turned slightly, brushing a strand of her hair behind her ear.

"Mina," he whispered, "you're safe now. With me. In this life."

Her eyes glistened.

She whispered back:

"I believe you."

Leon leaned his head lightly against hers.

They stayed like that—
not kissing,
not claiming,
not rushing—
but existing in the quiet, sacred space between two souls who had waited centuries to sit beside each other without fear.

As the night deepened, Mina drifted into a gentle sleep against his shoulder.

Leon remained awake.

He watched her with an expression that carried the weight of five hundred years—
love, loss, longing, recognition, and the fragile hope that this time,
finally,

they would not be torn apart.

He whispered into her hair, barely audible:

"Goodnight, Mina... My unfinished truth."

And for the first time in centuries, the night held them gently.

Two souls, reunited.
Two lives, aligned.
A love once broken, now beginning again—
slowly,
carefully,
truly.

Chapter 15: The Night of the First Dream Together

Leon did not move for a long time.

Mina slept with her head on his shoulder, breathing softly, peacefully—
a kind of peace that felt earned, not merely given.
The kind of peace a soul finds only after centuries of wandering.

He memorized the quiet of her face,
the way her fingers lightly curled into the fabric of his sleeve,
the faint trace of warmth her breath left against his neck.

When her breathing deepened, he exhaled and leaned his head back against the couch, finally letting fatigue reach him.

The kettle clicked in the kitchen.
The window hummed softly with the winter wind.
The room dimmed into shadows.

Leon closed his eyes.

He expected darkness.

But the moment sleep touched him—

the world shifted.

He opened his eyes into a soft brightness—
morning light filtering through thin linen curtains,
dust drifting like golden snow,
the smell of warm oil and wood and a faint sweetness in the air.

He wasn't on the couch.

He wasn't in Paris.

He was standing—
in the Renaissance studio.

Fully formed.

Fully present.
No blurring of edges.
No half-built memories.

His breath caught.

Then he heard it—
not the creak of a floorboard,
not the flutter of a curtain,
but the unmistakable sound of someone breathing behind him.

He turned slowly.

Mina stood in the doorway.

Not the Mina of modern Paris—
but the Mina from the past.

Her hair darker, braided softly.
Her dress simple but elegant.
Her face radiant with the quiet glow of someone who had come early,
arrived before she was expected,
drawn not by duty
but by the gravity of the man she loved.

She saw Leon.
Not the painter from before.
Leon—modern Leon.

Recognition rippled across her features.

"Leon?" she whispered.

His breath shook.
"Mina... you're here."

She stepped forward.
"Are you dreaming this?"

"I think so. But it doesn't feel like a dream."

"No," she whispered, "it doesn't."

She lifted her hand and touched the wooden table beside her.
Her fingers sank into the texture of it.
A real sound echoed—soft, solid, unmistakable.

Leon stepped toward her.

"We're in the same dream," he said slowly. "Not separate. Not parallel."

"Together," she finished.

Their hearts beat in unison—
slow, steady, ancient.

She walked toward the center of the room. Her steps made tiny sounds on the wooden floor. The sunlight drifted across her face, warming her skin.

Then she stopped suddenly.

Leon reached her side.

"What is it?"

She pointed.

On the easel stood the unfinished panel—
but not the one from the museum basement.

This version was more complete.

The eyes were sharper.
The shadows more defined.
The lips held a hint of a smile—
not yet formed,
not yet alive,
but closer.

Much closer.

Mina inhaled sharply.

"He... you... had done more than I remembered."

Leon stared at the brushstrokes, transfixed.

The pigments shimmered faintly, as if the painting itself were breathing.

He spoke softly.

"This is the moment before the end."

A soft tremor ran through Mina.

She nodded.
"I remember this. The afternoon light... the quiet... the way he asked me to sit even though he was sick."

Leon's hand moved to hers, instinctively, protectively.

The room deepened around them, their awareness sharpening as if they were truly reliving the moment, not merely observing it.

Then—

a sound.

A cough.

Weak.
Strained.
Painful enough to break Mina's breath in the present.

She clutched Leon's arm.

"He's here," she whispered.

The painter stepped into view—
not fully solid, but not transparent either.
He looked younger than he had in her memory.
Not the dying version.
A version from *just before*—
when he still believed he had enough time.

He didn't see them.

He moved toward the easel, adjusting his brush, leaning in to study the half-formed smile.

Mina exhaled a trembling sound.

Leon whispered, "He doesn't feel us. We're watching a truth replay itself."

The painter spoke suddenly—
soft, intimate, private:

"Your smile frightens me, Mina."

The sound of his voice sent a shockwave through both of them.

Mina pressed a hand to her heart.

Leon steadied her.

The painter continued, unaware of them:

"I cannot shape it. Every stroke feels wrong. It is not a smile I can command. It is not a smile meant for the world. It is..."
He lowered his head.
"...a smile you give only when you look at me."

Mina's breath broke.

The painter lifted his hand to his chest, as if steadying his weakening lungs.

"I fear," he whispered, "that the smile is not unfinished because I failed... but because I loved you too much to imprison it."

He turned away from the canvas and sat slowly, painfully, at the wooden chair.

He spoke again—
more fragile this time.

"I do not know if I will finish this painting. But if I do not... I pray that time will carry the rest."

Leon felt a tightness rise in his throat.

Mina's tears fell silently.

Then something impossible happened.

The painter lifted his head—

and this time,
he looked directly at them.

Both of them.

Leon's pulse froze.
Mina's breath stopped.

The painter should not have been able to see them.

But he did.

And recognition—
slow, profound, unshaken—
dawned in his eyes.

He rose slowly to his feet.

His voice trembled, but not from sickness.

"Ah," he whispered. "So this is how time keeps its promise."

Mina's knees weakened.
Leon held her upright.

The painter stepped closer.

He saw Leon first—
studied him with gentle sorrow
and gentle pride.

"You carry my hands," he murmured. "But you use them better than I ever could."

Leon's eyes burned.

Then the painter turned to Mina.

And his entire face softened.

"My Mina," he whispered.

Her breath fractured.
She took a step forward, tears streaming freely.

"I remember," she whispered. "I remember everything."

The painter smiled faintly—
not the broken smile of his last day,
but the smile of the man who had once loved her quietly, deeply, impossibly.

"I know," he said.

He lifted a trembling hand toward her.

Leon expected her hand to pass through it—
but it didn't.

Her fingers met his.

Warm.
Real.
Alive.

Time bent inward.

The studio dimmed.
Light folded.
The moment thickened.

The painter spoke one last time:

"It is finished now."

And then—

the studio dissolved.

The light collapsed into itself.

The Renaissance disappeared.

Mina woke with a soft gasp.

Her head still rested on Leon's shoulder.

But her hand—
her right hand—
was warm.

As if someone had held it
for real
in the place where dreams and memories met.

Leon woke too.

He looked at her, breath trembling.

"You saw him," he whispered.

She nodded slowly.

"And he saw us."

Leon exhaled—
a long, shaking breath
that seemed to release five centuries of unfinished longing.

Mina leaned her forehead against his.

"It's finished," she whispered.

Leon closed his eyes.

"No," he murmured, lifting her chin gently.
"It's beginning."

Chapter 16: The Portrait That Changes Overnight

Morning broke slowly over Paris, soft and gray, the kind of winter light that muted the city into a quiet watercolor. Mina woke before Leon—a small shift of breath, a faint rustle of fabric—and found herself curled against him on the couch, their bodies warm beneath the blanket he must have draped over them during the night.

She studied him for a moment.

He looked younger in sleep. Softer.
The weight of centuries seemed lifted from his face.

For the first time, she allowed herself to feel something without fear:
this is where I was always meant to wake up.

Leon's eyelids fluttered.

He opened his eyes slowly, as though surfacing from a dream he wasn't ready to leave.

The first thing he saw was her.

The faint smile that rose on his lips was quiet but unmistakably full.

"Good morning," he whispered.

Her cheeks warmed. "Hi."

He brushed a stray curl from her cheek.
It wasn't a gesture of romance—
it was recognition, tenderness, memory, and now something new forming inside the present.

They sat up slowly, still wrapped in the soft morning hush.

Mina tucked her knees under the blanket.
Leon rubbed his eyes with a quiet groan.

"How do you feel?" he asked.

She thought for a moment.

"Different," she said. "Like something rewrote itself inside me while I slept."

Leon nodded. "Me too."

They exchanged a quiet, knowing glance—the kind that belonged not to two people who had slept on a couch, but to two souls who had walked through a dream from another century and returned holding hands.

But then Mina's expression shifted—just slightly.

"Leon… something happened."

His posture sharpened. "What do you mean?"

"In the dream last night," she said carefully, "when he saw us… and when I touched him… it felt too real."

Leon's eyes deepened.

"It was real," he said. "I don't think those dreams are dreams anymore. I think they're… intersections."

Her throat tightened. "Between lives?"

He nodded once.

Silence filled the space between them—not emptiness, but charged, waking truth.

Then Leon stood.

"I need to go to the museum."

Mina blinked. "Why?"

He hesitated only a moment before answering.

"Because if last night was real… the painting might have changed."

She froze.

Her breath caught in her chest.

"You think the dream could affect the physical world?"

Leon turned toward her, his expression steady but filled with a fear-tinged wonder.

"Mina… time isn't a straight line, not for us. Not anymore. If we touched something there—really touched it—then something here may have shifted."

She swallowed hard. "We need to see it."

Leon nodded.

Mina slid out from beneath the blanket.
Leon handed her a spare sweater—soft, charcoal gray, far too big for her but warm.

She pulled it on.

It smelled faintly like him.

They left his apartment and walked in silence through the morning streets toward the Louvre. The city felt different—still itself, but layered now, as if the Paris of 500 years ago walked beside them in invisible footprints.

When they reached the staff entrance, Leon used his access card.
Mina followed him through the familiar corridors.

But today, every step felt heavier.
Not with dread—
with expectation.

When they reached the archive room, Leon paused before entering.

His voice was barely a whisper.

"Are you ready for whatever's inside?"

Mina took his hand.
"Yes."

He opened the door.

The temperature-controlled air drifted around them.

He crossed the room in steady, cautious steps.

He placed both hands on the metal rail of the storage rack.

Then he pulled.

The panel slid out.

Mina gasped.

Leon's breath left his body in a single sharp exhale.

The painting had changed.

Not dramatically.
Not obviously to anyone else.
But to them?

Undeniably.

The woman's left eye—
the one that had been no more than a charcoal suggestion—
was now unmistakably more defined.

The faint shading beneath it had deepened.
The arch of the brow was clearer.
Subtle warmth touched the corner of the eyelid.

And the smile—
still incomplete—
held the faintest new curve
as if a living expression had tugged at it overnight.

Mina covered her mouth with a trembling hand.

"Leon..." Her voice shook. "It wasn't like this yesterday."

"No," he whispered. "It wasn't."

He stepped closer, eyes wide, heart pounding.

"This…" He touched the wooden edge gently. "This level of pigment change—this precision—it couldn't happen unless someone painted it."

Mina's throat tightened. "But no one touched it."

He shook his head slowly.

"No one alive now."

She stared at him.

He stared back.

The truth crystallized silently between them.

The dream had crossed the boundary.
The painter's hand—his own past hand—had finished something in the night that time had left undone.

He swallowed.

"There's more," Mina whispered.

Leon turned sharply. "What do you see?"

She stepped closer to the painting, leaning in carefully.

"There," she said, pointing at the lower right corner where the background wash met the faint outline of her dress. "A new brushstroke. Just one. But it's fresh. I can feel it."

Leon inhaled slowly, deeply, reverently.

"It's a marking," he said. "A continuation. A sign that the connection between us and… him is still open."

Mina's fingers trembled.

"Leon… does this mean the painting can finish itself?"

He looked at her—
with wonder,

with fear,
with something like awe.

"No," he said softly.

She frowned.

"Then what does it mean?"

"It means," he whispered, "that *we* have to finish it."

Her breath caught.

"In this life," Leon continued, stepping closer to her, "the story didn't end. It paused. And now—now that time has opened—we have a chance to complete what was interrupted."

Mina stared at the painting, tears welling.

"It's waiting for us," she murmured.

He reached for her hand, intertwining their fingers.

"No," he corrected gently.
"It's waiting for you."

Mina blinked. "For me?"

Leon nodded slowly.

"You were the unfinished smile," he said. "Not the painting. Not the brushstroke. *You.* And until your heart returned, the painting could not change."

She covered her mouth with her free hand, overwhelmed.

Leon cupped her cheek with his other hand.

"Mina," he whispered, "the painting changed because you remembered. Because you touched him. Because time recognized your soul."

Her tears spilled over.

"And now?" she whispered. "What do we do now?"

Leon leaned his forehead to hers.

"Now," he said softly, "we follow the path the painting shows us."

The faint new smile—half-formed, awakening—seemed almost to glow between them.

Their unfinished love
had begun
to finish itself.

Chapter 17: The Hidden Layer Beneath the Paint

Leon didn't let go of her hand as they stood before the unfinished panel—now subtly, undeniably changed. The brushstroke that hadn't been there the day before shimmered faintly under the soft archival lighting, as if the pigment itself remembered being touched.

Mina felt a pulse of warmth in her chest, the same warmth she felt when the painter had held her hand in the dream.
The past and present were no longer separate rooms.
They were doorways opening into each other.

Leon stepped back with a slow, thoughtful breath.

"I need to see what's under the surface," he said.

Mina blinked. "Under the paint?"

He nodded, the intensity in his expression sharpening.
"I've never done a full imaging scan on this piece. There was no reason to. It was dismissed as incomplete. But now..." He looked at her. "Now everything is different."

"Will it hurt the painting?" she asked softly.

"No," he said. "We'll use multispectral imaging. X-ray, infrared. Completely safe."

He paused.

"And if there's something beneath this layer—another drawing, another portrait— we'll see it."

Mina's breath caught.

"You think he painted something else before this?"

Leon's voice lowered.

"I think he painted *you* twice."

A shiver ran through her.

The imaging lab was three floors above, behind a secured door with a card reader. Leon led her there quickly, purpose in every step. Mina followed close, pulse racing with a strange mix of fear and certainty.

Inside, the room smelled faintly of metals and old electronics. Machines hummed softly. Screens glowed. A large imaging scanner stood at the center, shaped like a ring surrounding an adjustable platform.

Leon placed the panel carefully at the center of the scanner.

Mina watched him handle it—not like a curator with an object, but like someone touching a memory in physical form.

He looked up at her.

"You stay beside me," he said gently.

She nodded.

He lowered the ring-shaped scanner.

Lights inside shifted to a dim red.

The machine whispered to life—soft clicking, a slow moving hum.

The first imaging pass began.

An outline appeared on the screen—clean, skeletal, showing wood grain and nail placements.

The second pass—infrared—revealed underdrawings, subtle shifts beneath the visible brushstrokes.

But it was the third pass—a deep X-ray composite—that made Leon inhale sharply.

A faint second image began forming under the main portrait.

Mina stepped closer, her heart pounding.

The layer beneath was rougher, bolder.
Not graceful like the surface.

Emotionally charged.
Immediate.

Leon adjusted the contrast.

And the image sharpened.

A woman.

Not posing.
Not sitting.
Not arranged.

Looking directly at the painter.

Her expression was nothing like the soft, serene face of the unfinished panel.
This face was alive—
eyes fierce with something unspeakable,
mouth parted slightly as if caught in the middle of a confession
or a promise
or a moment that could not be painted again.

Her hair was loose around her shoulders.
Her posture was closer, intimate, almost breathlessly so—
as if she had stepped toward the painter instead of sitting for him.

Mina's knees nearly buckled.

"That's me," she whispered.

Leon stared, stunned, reverent, speech frozen in his throat.

Mina pressed her hand to her chest.

"I remember this," she said, voice breaking. "This moment. It wasn't a sitting session.
It wasn't for a portrait. This was…"

She took a trembling step back.

Leon looked at her quickly. "Mina?"

"It was the day before he fell sick," she murmured. "I had gone to see him early, before he began painting. He wasn't ready. He wasn't expecting me."

Her voice softened to a fragile echo.

"He looked up from his work... and I stepped toward him. Not to pose. Just... because I couldn't help it."

Leon swallowed hard.

"And he painted you like that?" he asked.

"No," she whispered. "He *started* to. He sketched it, painted a few strokes... and then he covered it. He said it was too honest. Too raw. Too much of the truth."

Leon turned back to the imaging monitor.

He understood.

This wasn't a formal portrait.
It wasn't art.
It was love caught off guard.

He zoomed in on the eyes.

Mina flinched.

Because they weren't looking at the painter.
Not exactly.

They were looking at Leon.
At who he had been then.
At who he was now.

A person held inside time.

Mina touched the edge of the screen with trembling fingers.

"Why did he hide this?" she whispered.

Leon's voice was low, careful.

"Because it wasn't meant for the world."

She closed her eyes.

"He couldn't show this version of me to anyone," she whispered. "It wasn't the woman society wanted. It was the woman *he* knew."

Leon nodded.

"And the woman he loved."

Mina pressed her fist to her mouth, trying not to cry.

The rawness of the hidden portrait felt like a declaration across centuries.

Not ordered.
Not requested.
Not posed.

Real.

Vulnerable.

True.

She whispered:

"I didn't know he saw me like this."

Leon turned toward her, expression softening into something deeper.

"He saw you," he said, "the way I see you."

Her breath caught painfully.

Leon continued, quietly:

"And maybe... the way you've never seen yourself."

She looked at him—eyes glassy, wide, overwhelmed.

"Leon..."

He stepped closer, lifting her chin gently.

"You weren't just a muse," he said. "You weren't just a sitter. You were the truth he wasn't allowed to paint. So he buried it beneath the surface, hoping time would reveal it."

She trembled.

"And now," Leon whispered, "time has."

Mina's tears finally fell—slow, steady, silent.

Leon pulled her into a soft embrace, her forehead pressing into the crook of his neck.

She clutched his shirt.

"It's like he left this for us," she whispered.

"He did," Leon said. "He wanted you to see how he loved you. How I loved you."

She closed her eyes, letting the truth settle in her bones.

Leon rested his chin on her hair.

"We're not just remembering," he murmured. "We're reclaiming."

Mina inhaled shakily.

"He painted the part of me I thought no one saw."

Leon's arms tightened around her.

"I see her," he whispered.

The screen behind them glowed with the hidden portrait—
the raw truth beneath the layers,
the intimate version of Mina that time tried to bury but love insisted on saving.

And for the first time in five hundred years,
she was finally seen.

Chapter 18: When the Past Speaks Aloud

The lab was silent, except for the gentle hum of the imaging machine cooling down.
But the silence didn't feel empty—
it felt suspended, as if the air itself had stopped to listen.

Mina stood in Leon's arms, tears drying slowly on her cheeks.
Behind them, on the monitor, the hidden portrait continued glowing in grayscale:
the truest version of her, staring forward with a raw, unguarded intensity.

Mina pulled back slightly, her breath unsteady.

"Leon... I need to hear his voice again."

Leon nodded, brushing her cheek with his thumb.
"I think... we might."

He turned back to the console.

"We'll run a deep-pass scan," he said. "A layered composite. It's normally used to map pigment density, but sometimes—"

He hesitated.

Mina stepped closer. "Sometimes what?"

Leon exhaled slowly.

"Sometimes the scanner picks up anomalies... things embedded into the material. Fingerprints. Pressure indentations. Scratches. Even faint sound vibrations captured in the wood."

Mina's eyes widened.
"Sound?"

"It's rare," he said quietly. "Almost impossible. But not entirely."

Her pulse quickened.

"Let's try," she whispered.

Leon initiated the deep scan.

The room dimmed as the machine's internal lights shifted to a deep, resonant blue.

A soft vibration spread through the floor—gentle, consistent, almost like a heartbeat.

Mina stepped closer to the panel, unable to help herself.

As the scanner traveled across the surface, lines of spectral data appeared on the screen—color maps, density plots, waveforms.

Then something unusual began to form.

A waveform that wasn't noise.

Not environmental.
Not mechanical.

A pattern.

A repeating one.

Leon froze.

"That's not normal," he whispered.

Mina's fingers curled around the edge of the table.

"What is it?"

Leon zoomed in.

The waveform sharpened.

"It looks like…"
His voice faltered.
"…a voice signature."

Mina's knees weakened.

"Can we hear it?"

Leon hesitated for half a second—not because he doubted the possibility, but because hearing the voice of a man dead for centuries felt like crossing a threshold neither of them could return from.

Finally, he pressed a key.

The room fell silent.

The waveform began to play.

Static at first.
Soft cracks.
A distant hum.

Then—

A faint exhale.
A real one.
Human.

Mina's hand flew to her mouth.

Leon grabbed her other hand instinctively.

A whisper followed—fragile, wavering, but unmistakably human.

Italian.
Renaissance Italian.
Soft, breathless, intimate.

Leon increased the clarity.

And the words emerged:

"...non finisco... perché lei non è finita..."

Mina trembled violently.

"What does it mean?" she whispered.

Leon translated, voice shaking:

"'I do not finish... because she is not finished.'"

Mina's eyes filled again—
but with something more than grief.
With awe.
Recognition.
A trembling, ancient truth.

The recording crackled again.

Another whisper:

"...quando tornerà... seguirà la luce..."

Leon translated:

"'When she returns... she will follow the light.'"

Mina stared at the painting, breath ragged.

"Leon... he knew. He *knew* I would come back."

The scanner crackled once more.

This time, the whisper was softer, strained, as if spoken from a bed of illness, from a body failing but a love refusing to fade.

The voice said:

"...lei troverà l'uomo che è stato me..."

Leon closed his eyes.

"He said... 'She will find the man who was me.'"

Mina pressed her forehead into Leon's shoulder, breaking into soundless tears.

Leon wrapped both arms around her, holding her as the whisper played once more:

"...e allora, la nostra vita continuerà..."

Leon translated quietly:

"'And then, our life will continue.'"

Mina sobbed softly into his chest.

The recording ended.

The room fell utterly still.

For a long moment, neither of them moved.

Leon's hand stroked Mina's back slowly, grounding her, anchoring her to the present while the past washed over them like a tide older than the city surrounding them.

Finally, Mina pulled away enough to look at him.

"Leon," she whispered, her voice trembling, "he wasn't talking about the painting."

Leon's breath hitched.

"No," he said softly. "He wasn't."

"He was talking about *us*."

Leon nodded.

Mina touched the panel with the gentlest motion, fingers hovering just above the wood.

"He embedded his voice into the strokes," she whispered. "Into the pressure of his hand. Into the way he layered the paint. Like he was trying to leave a message for me that time couldn't erase."

Leon watched her with a depth of emotion he didn't hide.

"And you finally heard it," he said.

Mina closed her eyes.

"And you," she added softly, "were the part of the message I didn't know how to read."

A shiver moved through Leon—not cold, but the awakening of truth.

"Mina…"

She stepped closer, touching his chest with trembling fingers.

"He wasn't just leaving something for me. He was leaving something for *you*."

Leon swallowed hard.

"He said I would be the man who was him," Leon whispered incredulously. "But I never believed—"

She placed her hand over his heart.

"You are," she said simply. "And he knew I would recognize you."

Leon's eyes burned.

"And he knew," she added, her voice breaking, "that you would recognize *me*."

Leon lowered his forehead to hers.

Two breaths.
Two centuries.
Two lives merging.

The scanner lights dimmed.

The painting glowed faintly.

Between them, in a whisper softer than a sigh, Mina said:

"It's not just unfinished love, Leon."

He opened his eyes slowly.

"It's returning love."

Chapter 19: The Echo That Doesn't Belong to the Past

The imaging machine was powering down, its hum fading slowly into the thick, electrified stillness of the room.
Mina and Leon stood close—her forehead still touching his, his hands lightly around her waist—as if either feared the connection would dissolve if they moved too quickly.

But neither of them noticed something strange:

The monitor was still recording.

A thin red bar pulsed softly at the bottom of the screen—
Recording Active
—though Leon had not activated any audio capture manually.

Mina felt it first.

A subtle shift.
A sensation, not in the air but deeper—
like the room had inhaled.

She pulled back slightly, frowning.

"Leon... do you feel that?"

Leon opened his eyes and looked at her, confused—until he felt it too.
A pressure.
A low vibration.

Not physical.
Not mechanical.

Something else.

He turned toward the monitor.

The waveform that had stored the painter's whispers appeared again—
but this time
a new line began forming beneath it.

A fresh waveform.
Sharper.
More rhythmic.
Decidedly not from the Renaissance layer.

Leon froze.

"That wasn't there before."

Mina's pulse spiked. "Is it the same voice?"

Leon swallowed. "No."

He increased the sound clarity.

The waveform expanded.

The shape was unfamiliar—modern, clean, stable.
Not strained like the painter's dying breath.
Not torn by time.

A voice began to emerge—

but it wasn't from the past.

It was too clear.
Too crisp.
Too close.

Mina grabbed Leon's sleeve.

"Play it."

Leon hesitated—
because something in his body, his instincts,
was already warning him
that whatever they were about to hear
was not meant for the century behind them,
but the century ahead.

Finally, he clicked "PLAY."

Static.

A soft hum.

Then—

A woman's voice.

But not Mina's.

A voice that trembled, not with age, but with emotion:

"...if you're hearing this... it means I succeeded."

Mina's stomach dropped.

Leon's heart slammed into his ribs.

The voice continued:

"...I don't know what year it is for you. I don't know how the timelines have aligned. But I know this: love does not end. It travels."

Mina's breath hitched.
Her fingers dug into Leon's arm.

"Leon..." she whispered. "That's not a historical voice. That's..."

"Modern," he said.

The voice resumed—steady, urgent, aching:

"...you don't know me. Not yet. But I know you."

Mina felt a cold shiver glide down her spine.

Leon stepped closer to the monitor.

The voice inhaled shakily.

"...you are Mina. You are Leon. And I am what comes after you."

A silence so sharp it almost hurt filled the room.

Mina whispered, terrified:

"After us? What does that mean?"

The voice answered, as if hearing her:

"...I'm your daughter."

Mina's knees nearly gave out.

Leon caught her.

The voice continued—quiet, raw, urgent:

"...not born yet. Not in your lifetime. But in the one after that... the path you're opening now is the one I follow later."

Leon felt the world tilt.
Mina pressed both hands to her mouth.

The voice trembled again:

"...every lifetime you've tried to find each other. Every time you came close, something separated you. Until now. Until this moment. Until this bridge between centuries finally opened."

Leon whispered, disbelieving:

"She's speaking from... the future?"

Mina's voice cracked.

"Why would our daughter speak to us now?"

The voice softened.

"...because you're not finished. Not yet. You'll think you are. You'll think this reunion is the end of your story. But it's the beginning of mine."

Tears spilled from Mina's eyes.

Leon stood frozen—
every instinct, every breath hanging on the next sentence.

The voice lowered to a whisper:

"...I found the panel. Centuries after you. I found the truth you're discovering now. But I found something you haven't."

Leon stepped closer.

"Something we haven't?"

The voice seemed to steady itself—
as though bracing to reveal something heavy.

"...there is a second painting."

Mina gasped.

Leon's heartbeat roared in his ears.

The voice went on:

"...hidden. Lost. Forgotten. The one he painted of the two of you—not just her. Both of you. Together. It was taken. It was kept away because it wasn't proper. Because it was too intimate."

Mina staggered back, breath shuddering.

"A painting of *both* of us?"

Leon whispered, "It exists..."

The voice trembled now—barely holding together:

"...and you must find it. Because without it, your story cannot complete. And without your completion—mine... cannot begin."

A sharp crack of digital distortion broke the recording.
The voice fractured—
once, twice—

then returned for a final whispered plea:

"...please. Don't stop now. You're so close. Find the painting. Finish the story.
For you...
and for me."

The waveform collapsed.

The room fell silent.

Mina covered her face, shaking.

Leon reached for her, pulling her into his arms, feeling her whole body tremble with the impossible weight of what they'd heard.

Their daughter—
from the future—
had spoken to them.

And the message was clear:

Their love was not just a story returning—
it was a legacy beginning.

Leon held Mina tightly, whispering into her hair:

"We're not done. Not even close."

She sobbed against him.

He lifted her chin gently.

"We have to find the second painting."

Mina nodded, breath shaking.

"And finish everything," she whispered.

Together.

Chapter 20: The Museum That Never Shows Everything

Leon locked the imaging lab behind them, but the silence that followed wasn't peaceful—it was charged, humming with something too large for either of them to fully hold.

A voice from the future.
Their daughter.
A second painting.

Mina walked beside him down the hallway, but she wasn't fully in the hallway—part of her still stood inside the echo of that modern, trembling voice. The sound of it lived beneath her ribs, deep and haunting.

"Leon..." she whispered.
Her voice felt fragile.

He slowed.
"I know."

She stopped completely, turning toward him.

"Did we really just hear our daughter? Someone who... who doesn't exist yet? Someone born after we die?"

Leon's eyes softened, deepened.

"She exists," he said quietly. "Just not in our timeline. Not yet. But she exists."

Mina closed her eyes, trying to steady her breath.

Leon touched her elbow gently.

"You're not alone in this," he whispered. "Whatever is happening... we face it together."

She nodded, but her pulse was unsteady.

"What do we do now?"

Leon inhaled, slow and deliberate.

"We find the second painting."

He led her toward a part of the Louvre not shown on any public map—past doors marked for staff, past archival rooms no tourist would ever see, into a corridor with heavy wooden floors and older walls.

"This wing," Leon said softly, "contains records predating the French Revolution. Old inventories, confiscated works, paintings removed from estates during political transitions."

Mina listened carefully, her fingertips brushing along the rough wood of the wall.

"Are you saying," she murmured, "that the second painting was... taken?"

Leon nodded.

"Many works were. Some disappeared. Some reappeared. Some were 'lost,' though that usually meant someone hid them."

He stopped at a locked door with a brass plaque:

Restricted Archive — Pre-1700 Holdings
Access by Authorization Only.

Mina's breath hitched.
"Can we get in?"

Leon looked around.
Then he typed a code quickly, one Mina sensed he wasn't supposed to know.

The door clicked open.

He held it for her.

"After you," he whispered.

The archive was nothing like the modern storage rooms.

This one felt older—
dustier,

more intimate,
as if it carried secrets rather than artifacts.

Rows of wooden cabinets lined the room.
Bundles of brittle documents were tied with string.
Leather-bound inventories sat stacked like silent witnesses.

Mina stepped inside slowly.

The air smelled of parchment and age.

Leon went straight for a massive leather ledger on a central desk. The cover was cracked, the edges frayed. A date was stamped on the spine:

1685.

He opened it carefully.

Ink faded.
Columns of numbers.
Names of paintings and their estates.
Descriptions in archaic French.

"Look here," Leon murmured, pointing at a notation.
"'Portrait à deux figures – retiré.'"

Mina leaned in.

"'Two-figure portrait – removed.'"

Leon nodded.
"That's unusual. Renaissance artists rarely painted intimate dual portraits unless the subjects were married or politically symbolic."

He flipped pages with increasing urgency.

Mina scanned the lines.

Something was wrong.

"These entries..." she whispered, "why are some blacked out?"

Thick ink strokes covered several titles, including many marked "private," "sensitive," or "unsuitable."

Leon frowned.
"It looks censored. Possibly during the Revolution. Some works were hidden to protect them—or to hide them."

Mina's hand hovered over the page.

"Leon... what if ours is one of the censored ones?"

He didn't answer.

Because he found it.

A single line, halfway down the page, partly scratched out, partly legible:

Portrait interdit – femme inconnue & homme sans nom
Forbidden portrait – unknown woman & unnamed man

Beside it, in faint, smaller writing:

"expression trop intime pour exposition"
expression too intimate for display

Mina's stomach dropped.

"Leon," she whispered, "that's us."

His breath caught.

"It must be."

Mina felt a cold shiver touch her spine.

"Where did it go?" she whispered.

Leon scanned the next columns.

The location field was empty—scratched out deliberately.
The transfer field was likewise obliterated.

But two words remained—barely visible beneath the scraped ink.

Leon leaned closer, narrowing his eyes.

"It says… 'déplacé au sous-niveau.'"

Mina whispered the translation automatically:

"'Moved to the sub-level.'"

They exchanged a look.

A long, breathless silence followed.

The sub-level was the deepest part of the museum—below public reach, below staff reach—where confiscated or politically sensitive artworks were stored, often indefinitely.

Leon closed the ledger with trembling hands.

"We have to go there," he said.

Mina felt her pulse quicken.

"Is it allowed?"

"No," he answered simply. "But we still have to go."

She hesitated only a second.

"Then I'm going with you."

Leon reached for her hand and squeezed it once.

Not out of reassurance—
but agreement.

Partner to partner.
Soul to soul.
Past life to present life.

They stepped deeper into the archive.

Toward the elevator that led below the museum.
Toward the painting no one was meant to see.
Toward the truth their future daughter needed them to find.

As the elevator doors slid shut, Mina whispered:

"Leon... what do you think is in that painting? What did he paint of us?"

Leon looked at her, eyes dark with certainty and fear.

"Everything," he said.
"Everything we weren't allowed to finish."

The elevator began its descent—
quiet, slow,
as if lowering them into the heart of a story older than Paris itself.

Chapter 21 The Sub-Level of Forbidden Works

The elevator descended so slowly it felt intentional—as if the building itself was warning them, asking them to reconsider what they were about to uncover. The fluorescent light flickered once above their heads, then steadied.

Mina stood close to Leon, her hand wrapped around his.
Neither spoke.
They didn't have to.

Some truths required silence.

When the elevator finally stopped, a soft metallic chime echoed through the narrow chamber. The doors slid open onto a dim corridor lined with concrete walls and steel pipes. The temperature dropped instantly—cold enough that Mina inhaled sharply.

Leon stepped out first.

"This way," he murmured.

He knew the general layout—every curator did—but he'd never been down here. Almost no one had. The sub-level wasn't forbidden by sign, but by absence; no maps included it, no staff schedules listed it, no public tours acknowledged it existed.

It was the museum's buried heart.

Mina walked beside him, her breath faintly visible in the cold. The silence was so heavy it seemed to press against her ears. Only their footsteps broke it—soft, muffled, swallowed by the deeper quiet.

They reached a door with a rusted metal plate:

Dépôt 7 – Œuvres Retirées
Storage 7 – Withdrawn Works

Leon's hand hovered over the handle.

"It might be alarmed," Mina whispered.

Leon shook his head.

"If it were, we wouldn't have reached the elevator."

He pushed.

The door creaked open.

Inside was a long, windowless room lined with shelves and racks. Everything was shrouded in cloth, canvas, linen—objects the world had forgotten wrapped in layers of forced anonymity.

Mina stepped inside.

The cold deepened.
Her skin prickled.

Leon closed the door gently behind them.

"Where would it be?" she asked softly.

Leon scanned the racks, his eyes sharp and searching.

"Not near the front," he said. "If it was censored, it would be stored deeper. Away from easy reach."

They walked between the rows.

Some bundles were the size of small portrait frames; others rose taller than Mina's shoulders. A faint smell of aged oils and dust hung in the air.

Then—

Mina stopped.

A prickle ran across her spine.

"Leon," she whispered, "do you feel that?"

He turned. "Feel what?"

She stepped toward a specific rack without answering.
Her heartbeat quickened.
Her breath shortened.

It was as if something was pulling her—
not physically,
but unmistakably.

She reached a tall canvas wrapped completely in thick, yellowed linen, bound
around its edges with old cord. A hardened red wax seal secured the cord, cracked
at the surface but unbroken.

Leon joined her.

His breath caught.

The wax seal bore an emblem—
a stylized L intertwined with a serpent-like curve.

A curator's seal.

But not from the Louvre.

Leon whispered:

"This is from the royal inventory... before the Revolution."

Mina felt a tremor run through her entire body.

The canvas was the size of a full portrait—
large enough for two figures.
Large enough for the truth they had been denied.

Leon touched the linen gently.
The fabric was stiff, rough with age.

"This could be it," he murmured. "The forbidden portrait."

Mina reached out with a shaking hand, letting her fingertips brush the cold canvas
beneath the cloth.

The moment she touched it—

A shock raced up her arm.
A pulse—not painful, but deep, electric, familiar.
A sensation like déjà vu sharpened to a blade.

She gasped.

Leon grabbed her forearm instantly. "Mina!"

She shook her head, steadying herself.

"I'm okay—it's just…"
Her voice trembled.
"…this is it. I can feel it."

Her hand remained on the linen.

"And I think," she whispered, "I've touched it before."

Leon stared at her.

"You're remembering?"

She nodded slowly, eyes unfocused.

"Not clearly. Just… a feeling. A moment. A warmth."
Her voice dropped.
"A moment right after he said he loved me."

Leon ran a hand over the binding cord.

"It's sealed," he murmured. "Opening it might be dangerous. For the canvas. For us."

Mina stepped closer.

"Then we're careful."

Leon held her gaze.

"If we open this," he said softly, "everything changes."

Mina's throat tightened.

"Leon… everything already has."

He exhaled once, trembling.

"Help me turn it around," he said.

They gripped the edges of the wrapped canvas and gently rotated it. On the back, under layers of dust, faint ink was visible—handwritten, old, almost erased by time.

Mina brushed the dust away with trembling fingers.

The inscription emerged:

"Pour elle. Pour lui. Pour le temps qui nous reprendra."
For her. For him. For the time that will reclaim us.

Mina's breath faltered.

Leon froze.

There was no signature.

Just initials:

L. & M.

Mina's vision blurred with tears.

"It's ours," she whispered. "It has to be ours."

Leon nodded slowly.

"We open it," he said.

Together.

He took a small archival knife from a nearby tool table. Mina held the edge of the canvas steady as Leon carefully sliced the old cord. The wax seal cracked—not with a sharp sound, but a soft sigh, like something old releasing its final breath.

The linen loosened.

Leon hesitated.

"Mina... are you ready?"

She nodded, though her heart shook violently.

He pulled the cloth away.

The air rushed out of Mina's lungs.

Leon staggered back a step, stunned.

The painting beneath was—

Alive.
Raw.
Devastating.

The colors were rich, untouched by time thanks to the sealed wrapping. The brushstrokes vibrant, emotional, unmistakably belonging to a master's hand.

And there they were.

Not as lovers in embrace.
Not as painter and muse.

But as two souls facing one another.

Leon—the painter from centuries ago—stood on the left side of the composition, turned slightly toward her, painted with quiet strength, vulnerability in his eyes.

Mina, in Renaissance dress, stood on the right—but not posing.
Her hand reached toward him, not touching, but only a breath away.

The background was nothing but soft light, gold and pale blue, making the two figures glow as though painted in the moment before time intervened.

And at the bottom right corner, barely visible, written in faint pigment:

"La rencontre qui traverse les siècles."
The meeting that crosses centuries.

Mina's tears spilled, unstoppable.

Leon stepped closer, his hand covering his mouth.

He traced the outline of the male figure's face—
his face,
as it had been before.

"He painted us," Mina whispered, breath breaking. "Together. As we really were."

Leon nodded slowly, overwhelmed.

"This wasn't meant for the world," he murmured. "This was meant for us—when we returned."

Mina touched the edge of her painted face.
Her fingers quivered.

"It's the moment before everything fell apart," she said softly. "The moment we almost said everything. The moment we didn't get to finish."

Leon turned toward her.

"And now," he said gently, reverently, "we finally can."

They stood before the portrait—
two figures painted in another lifetime,
two souls reunited in this one.

And between them, the truth shone brighter than any museum light:

Their story was never lost.

It was waiting.

Chapter 22: The Night the Painting Breathes

They stood before the forbidden portrait for a long time, unable to speak.

Not because they had no words—
but because any word would have felt too small for what lay before them.

The painting—their painting—did not merely depict two figures.
It *remembered* them.

The colors were impossibly vivid for something centuries old.
The way the light fell between the two figures seemed almost alive.
The expressions... soft, longing, caught in the gravity of one unfinished moment.

Mina lifted a trembling hand toward the canvas.

"Leon... look at my eyes."

He did.

Painted-Mina stared at Painted-Leon with an intensity that almost hurt to witness—
raw recognition, devotion, fear, longing, and something even deeper:

a promise.

Leon whispered, "He captured the moment before you left the studio that final day."

Mina nodded.
"It was the last time I saw him alive."

Leon swallowed hard.

"I remember," she murmured. "I remember standing that close to him. I remember thinking... if I stay here one more second, I'll never be able to leave."

His chest tightened.

"And he painted that?"

"No," she whispered. "He started painting it before that day. But he finished it the night before he died."

Leon froze.

"How do you know that?"

She stepped closer to the canvas, fingertips hovering a hair's breadth from the painted light.

"Because I was there," she whispered.
"I returned to the studio after dark. I knew he was sick. I knew he shouldn't be working. I begged him to rest."

A shiver ran through her.

"I didn't know he was finishing *this*."

Leon touched her back gently.
"Mina..."

Her voice softened, trembling:

"He painted us... as we were... and as we were meant to be."

Leon couldn't speak.

The silence in the sub-level was thick, humming with the weight of centuries.

Finally, Mina stepped back.

"Leon... something's happening."

He frowned. "What do you—"

Then he saw it.

The painting breathed.

Not literally—
but the light inside it shifted.

Subtly.
Delicately.
As if someone had turned a dial inside the pigment.

The golden wash between the figures brightened and softened, pulsing faintly.

Mina's breath halted.

"Leon... the light wasn't like that a moment ago."

"No," he whispered. "It wasn't."

He looked around.
No lights were flickering.
No reflections from the hallway disturbed the scene.

The glow came from inside the painting.

Mina stepped closer, mesmerized.

"It's responding to us."

Leon's heartbeat quickened.

"To you," he corrected softly.

As they watched, the space between the painted figures—
that narrow breath of distance,
the moment before touch—
glimmered faintly, like heat rising from a candle flame.

Mina's lips parted.

"It's the moment that never happened," she whispered.

Leon looked at her.

"The moment before you touched."

She nodded slowly.

"The moment just before the story broke."

The light pulsed again—
faint, trembling—

and then stabilized.

Leon's hand brushed the lower edge of the frame.

"Mina?"

She didn't take her eyes from the painting.

"Yes?"

"There's something written here."

She knelt beside him.

At the very bottom of the frame, carved so faintly into the wood that it could only be seen under specific lighting, was a line of tiny script—Italian, handwritten, precise.

Leon read it aloud:

"Il tocco completa ciò che il tempo interruppe."
The touch completes what time interrupted.

Mina's breath caught in her throat.

"Leon..."

He looked at her, voice barely a whisper.

"He's telling us how to finish it."

"How?" she whispered.

Leon brushed his fingers along the carved words.

"It says the painting completes when the touch completes."

She froze.

Then turned slowly toward him.

"Leon... he painted us reaching for each other. But not touching."

He nodded.

"Because we never did, before he died."

Her eyes filled.
"So if we—"

She couldn't finish the sentence.

Leon stepped closer—
slowly,
carefully,
as though approaching something fragile and sacred.

"Mina," he whispered, "give me your hand."

She lifted it—shaking slightly—and placed it in his.

The moment their fingers touched, something shifted.

Not the painting—
the room itself.

A soft warmth radiated from their joined hands,
like the echo of another century sliding gently into this one.

Leon guided her hand toward the painting.

Their combined fingers hovered a few centimeters from the canvas surface.

Mina whispered:

"Are we really supposed to touch it?"

"No," Leon said.
"Not the painting."

Her breath hitched.

"Then what?"

Leon lifted their entwined hands—

—closer to the painted hands on the canvas.

Just before they brushed the surface,
he stopped.

"Here," he whispered.
"This is where time broke."

Mina's voice trembled.

"And if we complete the gesture now…?"

Leon's eyes softened.

"Then the painting finishes itself."

Their hands stayed suspended in the air—
their real touch echoing the almost-touch in the painting.

And then—

The painting's light pulsed,
brighter than before,
a soft golden bloom spreading through the canvas.

Mina gasped.

Leon squeezed her hand gently.

The painted figures—
or perhaps the light between them—
shifted, subtly, impossibly.

The distance between Painted-Leon and Painted-Mina
seemed to narrow
by the faintest breath.

Mina burst into tears.

"Leon… it's working."

"It's waking."

The light pulsed again.

The painting was not breathing—

it was remembering.

And for the first time in centuries,
the unfinished moment between them
began to draw its first unbroken breath.

Chapter 23: When the Canvas Opens Its Eyes

They didn't speak.
They didn't move.
For several seconds, the only thing alive in the sub-level vault was the faint golden radiance pulsing through the forbidden portrait—
a glow so delicate, so impossibly subtle, that anyone else might've dismissed it as imagination.

But not Mina.
Not Leon.

Because they both felt it.
Not with sight, but with the thin, trembling thread that bound their souls across centuries.

Leon finally released a breath he hadn't realized he was holding.

"Mina," he whispered, "we need to step back."

She nodded, still trembling.

He guided her away from the canvas—one step, two—until their hands fell naturally apart, though neither wanted them to.

The moment they separated, the light inside the painting dimmed.

Not vanished.
Just settled.
Like a heartbeat slowing after exertion.

Mina placed a hand over her chest.

"It feels alive," she whispered. "Like... like it's breathing."

Leon swallowed.

"It is."

She turned to him, startled. "What do you mean?"

He didn't answer right away. His gaze stayed fixed on the painting—studying not the brushstrokes, but the energy surrounding it.

"Mina," he said slowly, "this painting was sealed for centuries. No light. No air. No environment that could cause even natural pigment shifts. Yet... the colors changed."

Mina's pulse quickened.

"You mean—"

"It responded," Leon said. "To what we did."

She shivered.

"Leon," she whispered, "I think something else changed too."

"What?"

She stepped cautiously closer.
Not touching, not intruding—
just enough to study painted-Mina's eyes.

Her own painted gaze, which had been soft and longing mere hours before, had shifted by a fraction of a degree.
Barely visible.
But definite.

Painted-Mina was no longer looking solely at Painted-Leon.

Her eyes angled outward—
toward her.
Toward the real Mina standing in the vault.

As if the portrait had turned
in recognition.

Mina's breath cracked.

"Leon... she's looking at me."

Leon came to her side, squinting carefully.

At first glance, the painted expression appeared unchanged.
But the more he looked—
the more the shift became undeniable.

The painted gaze had deepened.
Focused.
Awakened.

"It's impossible," he murmured.

But impossibility had already lost meaning.

Mina's throat tightened.

"She's... seeing me," she whispered. "Not as memory. Not as muse. As... herself."

Leon turned to her sharply.

"What do you feel?"

She closed her eyes.

And the moment she did, something stirred inside her—
a pull, a ripple, a gentle pressure behind her breastbone,
as if a door she didn't know existed had creaked open.

"I feel..."
She swallowed.
"...like she's trying to tell me something."

Leon's voice softened.
"Try to listen."

Mina took a slow breath.

And then another.

Deep.

Steady.

Her fingers tingled.

Her vision blurred at the edges.
Not from tears, but from something shifting inside the room itself—
as if the air had grown denser, electric.

A faint whisper brushed her ear.

So faint she thought she imagined it.
But it came again.

A woman's voice.
Soft.
Warm.
Ancient.

"Non aver paura, amata mia..."
Do not be afraid, my beloved...

Mina jolted back with a gasp.

Leon grabbed her arms.

"Mina! What happened?"

She stared at him, breath shaking.

"She spoke."

Leon's eyes widened. "The painting?"

"No." Mina touched her chest. "*She.* The woman inside it. Me. The past me."

His grip tightened, grounding her.

"What did she say?"

Mina's lips trembled.

"She told me not to be afraid."

Leon exhaled—shaky, relieved, shaken.

"Mina... she's you."

She shook her head vehemently.

"No, Leon. She's not just me. She's the part of me that never lived her full story. The part that never touched you. The part that died with everything unspoken."

Tears gathered, but she blinked them back.

"And she's waking up."

Leon guided her to sit on a low wooden crate. She did, shakily. He stood in front of her, steady and warm.

"Tell me exactly what you felt."

"It wasn't a memory," she whispered. "It was immediate. Present. Like… like a second heartbeat inside me."

Leon took her hands.

"This connection—it's evolving."

Before she could respond, a soft sound echoed through the vault.

A whisper of linen shifting.

A breath of air where there should be none.

Leon turned sharply.

The painting was glowing again.

But this time the light gathered specifically in the painted Mina's eyes—
subtle, but undeniable.
A shimmer.
A deepening.
A soft, inner radiance.

Mina's real heart pounded hard.

"Leon… she's awake."

Leon stepped closer to the painting.

And then he froze.

"Mina," he whispered, "come here."

She hurried to him.

Her breath caught.

The painted version of herself—
the one from another lifetime—
was no longer looking outward.

She was looking directly at Mina.

Straight into her eyes.

Alive.
Silent.
Present.

Not trapped.
Not frozen.
Not merely depicted.

Recognizing.

Mina's breath trembled as a single tear slid down her cheek.

Leon placed a hand on her back.

"She sees you," he said softly.

"I see her," Mina whispered.

And for the first time in this life,
the woman she once was
and the woman she had become
stood face to face.

Two lifetimes

meeting in a single heartbeat.

The painting pulsed once more.
And then—
as if exhaling after centuries—
a faint new line appeared at the edge of the canvas.

Mina gasped.

Leon leaned in.

"Mina… that's—"

"A new brushstroke," she whispered.

It hadn't been there minutes ago.
Or hours ago.
Or centuries ago.

The painting was continuing itself.

And the next step was clear.

The past would no longer speak only through memory.
It was speaking directly through art.

Through her.

Through them.

And whatever came next
would change both their lives
—and time itself—
forever.

Chapter 24: The Mirror Stroke

The new stroke on the painting was so faint it could have been a shadow—
a soft line of warm gold tracing the edge of the background, curving in a direction
that didn't match any previous movement on the canvas.

But Mina knew—
the same way she knew her own breath—
that it had not existed before.

Leon crouched, eyes narrowed.

"This wasn't here. Mina... this is fresh pigment."

She knelt beside him.

"Impossible."

Leon shook his head slowly.

"Everything we've seen tonight is impossible."

He lifted a gloved finger and hovered it a millimeter from the new line—careful,
reverent.

"It's *wet*," he whispered.

Mina's stomach tightened.

Wet pigment.
On a sealed 500-year-old painting.

She swallowed. "Leon... what does it mean?"

He looked at her—eyes wide, voice low.

"It means the painting isn't just waking. It's *continuing*."

Mina felt dizzy.

The forbidden portrait wasn't finished in the past.

It was finishing itself now.
With them.

She reached instinctively for the frame, steadying herself—

But the moment her hand brushed the wood, she gasped and jerked back.

A sharp, tingling shock ran through her fingertips.
Not painful—
but intimate.
Recognizable.

Leon grabbed her wrist.
"Mina! What happened?"

She stared at her own skin, trembling.

"I felt... something. Not an electric shock. It felt like... like someone's hand touched mine from the other side."

Leon froze.

"The other side of what?"

"The canvas," she whispered.

Before he could process that, Mina lifted her hand to inspect the tingling spot.

Her breath stopped.

A small, thin line—
the same shape as the new brushstroke—
had appeared on her skin.

Golden.
Faint.
Barely visible.
But unmistakable.

Leon leaned in, eyes wide.

"That's... that's the same curve."

Mina's voice trembled.

"It's on me."

"It's *matching* the painting," Leon murmured, stunned. "A mirror stroke."

Mina stood abruptly, adrenaline flooding her limbs.

"Leon, this isn't just a painting reacting. This is a connection. Something is syncing between the canvas and—"

She touched her chest, breath unsteady.

"—and me."

Leon rose to his feet, hands steadying her shoulders.

"Tell me how it feels."

She closed her eyes.

The golden mark pulsed softly—
not with light, but with sensation.
A warmth spreading inward,
like a message forming beneath her skin.

"It feels like..."
She inhaled sharply.
"...like she's touching me."

Leon's breath faltered.

"She," he whispered. "The woman in the painting. The past you."

Mina nodded.

"She's reaching through it. Reaching to finish something. To communicate."

Leon's hands tightened on her arms.

"What is she trying to say?"

Mina listened—
not with ears,
but with the quiet center of herself.

"She wants me to follow," Mina whispered.

Leon stiffened. "Follow where?"

She opened her eyes, and they were different—
deeper, focused, lit from the inside.

"She's guiding me somewhere. Somewhere the painting remembers."

Leon glanced back at the portrait.

The painted Mina's eyes seemed even more alive now—
not just looking outward,
but urging, inviting, telling.

"We can't leave this here," Mina said suddenly.

Leon shook his head.
"Mina, it's a priceless artifact. We can't move it without—"

She turned to him sharply, her voice trembling but certain.

"Leon. Listen to me. The painting isn't just an artifact anymore. It's active. It's communicating. And something in it wants to take us further. We can't leave it here alone in the dark."

Leon stared at her, torn between reason and the undeniable truth of everything he'd witnessed tonight.

"Where would we even take it?" he whispered.

Mina stepped closer to the canvas.
The golden line on her skin pulsed again, faint but insistent.

"Somewhere with light," she murmured.
"Somewhere with space."

Leon looked around the vault—the cold concrete walls, the iron racks, the oppressive stillness.

"You mean the lab," he said. "The imaging room."

Mina nodded.

"It woke there. It'll wake again."

Leon hesitated.
Every curator instinct screamed that moving a forbidden royal painting without authorization was madness.

But his soul—
the part of him echoing across centuries—
felt the opposite.

He turned back to the painting.

The version of him—painted centuries ago—looked right at him now.
Not as a portrait,
but as a mirror.

Leon exhaled.

"Okay. We take it upstairs."

He reached for the frame, testing its weight.

Mina stepped beside him, helping lift it carefully.

As they carried the canvas out of the vault, Mina felt the golden mark warm again—
a steady pulse,
like a compass guiding her.

Down the hall.
Into the elevator.
Toward the lab.

Toward the next chapter in a story that had waited five hundred years to continue.

But as the elevator doors closed, Mina's heart lurched.

Because at the last second—
before the panel slid completely shut—
she glimpsed something in the dim vault reflection.

The painted Mina in the portrait had moved.

Just slightly.
Just enough.

Her hand—
the painted hand reaching toward the painted Leon—
was now a fraction closer.

The canvas was finishing itself.

And the past life she had once lived
was waking
moment by moment.

Chapter 25: The Lab of Second Birth

The elevator doors opened onto the quiet, fluorescent-lit hallway of the conservation wing.
Everything looked normal—sterile, orderly, rational—yet Mina felt the air trembling with something that did not belong to this century.

She and Leon carried the forbidden portrait carefully between them.

The weight didn't feel heavy.
It felt *alive.*

The golden mark on Mina's skin pulsed in a steady, warm rhythm—as if syncing with something inside the painting.

When they entered the imaging lab, Leon closed the door behind them and locked it.

For a moment, the room was silent.

Then Mina whispered, "Leon... it feels like the painting knows it's here."

He didn't laugh.
He didn't doubt her.

Because he felt it too—
a pressure in the air, a quiet hum, an expectancy.

He set the painting gently on the vertical stand.
Mina stood close, her hand unconsciously touching the golden line on her forearm.

Leon turned on the low-level ambient lighting first.

The painting reacted instantly.

A faint shimmer rolled across the canvas—
like light moving beneath water,
or breath moving beneath skin.

Mina stepped closer.
Her pulse hammered.

"Leon… it's stronger here."

Leon adjusted his gloves, his breath unsteady.

"We'll try a controlled scan. Low intensity. Just enough to see if the imaging picks up any changes."

Mina nodded, but her eyes never left the painting.

The imaging machine powered up with a low, resonant hum.
Nothing bright.
Nothing overwhelming.
Just a soft, glowing wash of spectral light.

The painting shimmered again.

But this time—
the shimmer didn't stay contained within the canvas.

A ripple of golden luminance drifted outward,
touching the floor,
the air,
the edges of their shadows.

Mina gasped and reached out instinctively.

"Mina—!" Leon grabbed her arm. "Don't touch it during the scan!"

But it was too late.

Her fingertips brushed the glowing air just inches from the canvas.

And the world broke open.

The lab vanished.

It didn't fade—
it *collapsed,*
like a sheet of fabric snapping into another shape.

Mina's breath caught in her throat as she found herself standing on cobblestone.

Damp.
Cold.
Smelling of river fog and wood smoke.

Paris.
But not the Paris she knew.

The Seine flowed darker, narrower, edged with wooden scaffolding.
Horse hooves clattered somewhere behind her.
A baker shouted in old French.
Smoke curled from chimneys shaped nothing like the modern skyline.

Mina staggered.

"Leon?" she whispered.

But her voice hit empty air.

She was alone.

Her hands trembled.
She lifted her arm—

The golden mark was still there, glowing faintly.

A sign.
A guide.

The past had pulled her back.

But not into a memory.

Into a *moment she never lived.*

Mina turned slowly.

And then she saw it.

A small studio window, candlelit from within.
Familiar.
Painfully familiar.

Her heart lurched.
Her feet moved before she could think.

She approached the door.
Her hand rose to knock—

Then she heard it.

A cough.
Weak.
Raspy.
Fragile.

Her breath broke.

She knew that sound.

She pressed her hand to the wood.

"Leonardo," she whispered.

Her voice cracked.

"Please... open the door."

But the door didn't open.
The world flickered—

And suddenly she was inside the studio.

Not by movement.
By memory being rewritten.

Leonardo—her past-life beloved—sat at the easel, weak and pale, a blanket around his shoulders. His brush trembled slightly with each stroke.

And on the easel was the forbidden painting.

Half-finished.

Her painted hand reaching toward his.

His painted hand reaching toward hers.

Leonardo glanced up—
and though he couldn't see her,
Mina felt the shift in the air.

He sensed something.
A presence.
A future.

He whispered, voice thin:

"Ti troverò di nuovo… in qualunque vita."
I will find you again… in any life.

Mina's knees weakened.

She reached for him—
but her hand passed through the air, unable to touch.

"No—no, please—"
She tried again, desperate.

But the moment her fingers neared his shoulder,
the world convulsed.

The studio wavered,
the floor tilting,
the colors swirling like wet paint sliding off canvas.

Mina screamed as the room exploded into gold light—

—and she crashed back into the imaging lab.

Her whole body jerked violently.
Leon caught her before she hit the floor.

"Mina! Mina, look at me—"

She gasped, clawing at her chest.

"Leon—he was—he was dying—he was finishing the painting—he knew—he said—
"

Leon held her firmly.

"What did he say?"

Tears spilled from her eyes.

"He said he would find me again. In any life."

Leon's breath caught.

The imaging machine beeped sharply.

They turned.

The painting had changed.

Not subtly.
Not faintly.

The formerly unfinished area—
the space between the two painted hands—
was now nearly filled in.

A new brushstroke glistened.
Fresh.
Wet.
Impossible.

Leon walked toward it slowly.

"Mina," he whispered, awe breaking through his voice,
"you didn't just see the past."

She wiped her tears with shaking hands.

"What did I do?"

"You *completed* it. Not with paint. With what was missing from that moment."

Mina stared.

"Love," Leon whispered.

Mina turned to him.

"No, Leon. Not love. Not just that."

Her voice steadied, eyes shining with something ancient and new at the same time.

"Presence."

Leon's breath stilled.

Because deep inside, he knew she was right.

The painting wasn't finishing itself through pigment.

It was finishing itself through time—
through the rejoining of souls that had once been torn apart.

"Leon..." she whispered.

"Yes?"

Her voice trembled.

"I think this painting is the bridge between our lives."

"And the bridge," Leon said softly, "is waking."

They stared at the canvas, breathless.

Because the hands—
the painted hands—
were only a hair's width from touching now.

Just one more unbroken moment.

One more step.

One more truth.

And the past would meet the present
in the only place time cannot break—

the space where souls recognize each other.

Chapter 26: When the Hands Finally Touch

The lab was silent.
But not peaceful.

It was the silence of a world holding its breath.

The forbidden portrait stood on the easel, golden light flickering faintly within its surface like embers refusing to die. The two painted figures—Leonardo and the woman Mina once was—now reached for each other with only the smallest impossible distance remaining between their fingers.

One brushstroke.
One moment.
One heartbeat.

Mina stood before it, her entire body trembling.
The fresh golden line on her arm still glowed softly—no longer faint, but warm, pulsing in rhythm with her real heartbeat.

Leon hovered beside her, stunned by what he'd just witnessed—
her collapse,
her journey into the past,
her return with a living memory no historical document could ever contain.

"Mina," he whispered, "we need to understand what happened before we go any further."

But she shook her head slowly.

"You don't understand," she said softly. "It's not waiting for us to understand. It's waiting for us to *finish*."

Leon swallowed hard.

"What exactly needs finishing?" he asked, though his voice betrayed that he already knew.

Mina lifted her glowing arm, fear and wonder mixing in her eyes.

"The moment," she whispered. "The moment that never happened. The moment that cost us centuries."

Leon turned to the painting again.

The hands—
one hers, one his—
paused in eternal almost-touch.

It hurt to look at.
Not as an artwork—
but as a memory so unfinished it had become a wound.

Mina's voice shook.

"I saw him. In his studio. He was painting this. He was dying, Leon—he could barely breathe—but he finished it for me. For us. And it wasn't enough. Time stole the rest."

Leon took her hand gently.

"What do you feel now?"

She closed her eyes.

"A pull," she whispered. "Like something inside the painting... or something inside *me*... wants to complete the gesture."

Leon glanced back at the canvas.

"Mina... if the painting is reacting to us—if it's alive in some way—then finishing it might trigger something we can't anticipate."

Her eyes opened. Steady. Certain.

"Leon," she whispered, "everything that's happened was impossible. We're beyond the point of caution."

He let out a breath.

Then nodded.

"How do we finish it?"

Mina turned toward him fully.

"You help me."

Leon swallowed. "How?"

She lifted her hand—
the one with the golden mark.

"You take my hand," she whispered.
"And we touch the place where their fingers almost meet."

He froze.

"Mina... if we physically touch the painting—"

"It won't damage it," she said.

"How do you know?"

She stepped closer to him.

"Because I am the painting. And so are you."

The truth struck him deep, like a bell's resonance inside his ribcage.

He placed his hand in hers.

Their fingers intertwined.

Their palms pressed together.

The golden mark on her arm flared softly, as if in approval.

They faced the canvas—
two souls before their past selves,
reborn in the only life where they both survived long enough to meet again.

"On three," Mina whispered.

Leon nodded.

"One..."

The painting shimmered faintly.

"Two..."

Their joined hands trembled in the glowing air.

"Three."

They reached forward.

Their fingers did not touch the pigment.

They didn't have to.

The moment their joined hands hovered a breath away—

The painting came alive.

A burst of golden radiance flared from the canvas, exploding outward in total silence. The air rippled like water struck by a stone. The lab dissolved into streams of light. The temperature dropped. Then rose. Then vanished entirely.

Mina screamed—but the scream had no sound.
Leon staggered, gripping her hand as the world buckled.

And the painting—

The painting moved.

The two painted hands—hers and his—
closed the final distance
and touched.

The instant they met, a shockwave of golden light burst from the canvas, enveloping Mina and Leon. The floor vanished beneath their feet. The ceiling evaporated. The machines dissolved.

There was no lab.

No museum.
No time.
No separation.

Only a rush—
a flood—
a collapsing of centuries all at once.

Mina fell to her knees, gasping, gripping Leon's arm with desperate fingers.

"Leon—!"

He fell with her, arms around her, holding her as the golden light wrapped around them like a living storm.

Then—
through the blinding brilliance—
a shape formed.

The painting was no longer still.

It was a doorway.

A threshold.

A trembling veil between lifetimes.

And through it—

A figure stepped forward.

A man.
Warm eyes.
Renaissance clothing.
Familiar in a way that tore her heart open.

"Leonardo..." Mina whispered, breaking.

But the figure shook his head gently.

Not Leonardo.
Not exactly.

The same soul.
The same eyes.
But younger.
Clearer.
Unburdened by the illness that had claimed him.

It was the version of him that lived in the painting—
unfinished until this moment.

Mina reached toward him instinctively, tears streaming.

Leon squeezed her hand, trembling with awe.

The painted man smiled softly—
a smile neither of them had seen in 500 years.

"Mina," he whispered, "I've been waiting."

Her heart fractured with recognition.

"Why… why now?" she sobbed.

He stepped closer.

"Because now," he whispered, "you finally touched what time broke."

He lifted his hand.

"Come."

Mina tensed.

Leon held her tightly.

The Renaissance version of him looked at Leon—really looked at him—and nodded
with deep understanding, as if acknowledging:

I am you.
You are me.
We are the same soul across different lives.

Leon's chest tightened.

Mina stared at the glowing threshold, trembling.

"If I step through… do I leave this life?"

He shook his head gently.

"No. The door only opens to give you what you lost. Not to take anything from you."

Mina sobbed once, overwhelmed.

"What did I lose?"

His eyes softened.

"A goodbye."

A silence deeper than any night settled around them.

Leon whispered into her hair:

"I'm right here. Whatever you choose, I'm with you."

She turned toward the light, reached out—

And stepped forward.

The golden doorway flared.

The Renaissance man reached for her gently.

Their hands touched—

And the world turned white.

Chapter 27: The Goodbye That Never Happened

The white light softened—
not fading,
but *changing*,
thickening into warmth, shaping itself into a room she knew yet did not know.

A studio.

His studio.

But not as Mina last saw it in her vision...
not cold, not shadowed by illness, not dimmed by approaching death.

This studio was filled with morning light—
soft, golden, alive.
The windows were open.
A breeze carried the scent of linseed oil and early spring.

And there he stood.

The man she had loved in another century.
Not a ghost.
Not a memory.
Not a painting.
But himself—healthy, whole, radiant in a way she had never been allowed to see.

Leonardo.

The version of him before he became ill.
The version of him she never got the chance to say goodbye to.

His eyes softened the moment he saw her.

"Mina."

Her heart shattered.

She pressed a hand to her mouth, tears spilling immediately.

"I don't—"

Her voice broke.
"I don't understand… how are you here? How am I here?"

Leonardo stepped closer, slow, reverent, like approaching a miracle he feared might vanish.

"You came because you touched the moment we never finished," he said gently. "And that opened the door."

She lifted a trembling hand toward his face, terrified he might dissolve.

He didn't.

Her fingertips brushed the warm line of his jaw.

He closed his eyes, leaning into her touch with a breath that sounded like centuries of longing released in one exhale.

"Oh," she whispered, "you're real."

"As real as the love that brought you back to me," he murmured.

She wept—quiet, shaking, undone.

He took both her hands, kissing them softly, as if memorizing the shape he had missed across lifetimes.

"Mina," he said, voice thick with emotion, "I have waited so long to finish this moment with you."

A sob caught in her throat.

"I saw you," she whispered. "Finishing the portrait. Sick. Alone. I tried to reach you but—"

He pressed a finger gently to her lips.

"That was the past," he said. "And the past is not where goodbyes belong."

She shook her head, tears falling.

"I never got to tell you—"

"Nor I, you," he said softly.

His thumb stroked her cheek.

"We were torn apart before we could speak the truth aloud."

She leaned into him, forehead touching his chest, tears soaking his shirt.

"I loved you," she whispered.
"I loved you so much it burned me. And I was so frightened. I thought if I didn't leave, I would lose myself. But leaving meant losing you instead."

His breath trembled.

"I knew," he murmured into her hair. "I knew you loved me. Even as you walked away, I felt it. And I never blamed you. Not once."

She sobbed harder.

He lifted her chin gently.

"When the end came for me," he said, voice soft as feathers, "my last thought was not regret. It was you."

Her knees weakened; he held her firmly.

"And I promised myself," he continued, "that if souls are real, if time is kind, I would find you again. Or I would wait until you found me."

She closed her eyes, tears falling freely.

"I'm here," she whispered. "I found you."

"No," he corrected gently.
"You *returned.* For me. For us."

She touched his face again, as if anchoring every breath, every detail.

"Why did this doorway open now?" she asked softly.

He smiled—a sad, luminous smile.

"Because there was something we never finished. Something the soul remembers even when the mind forgets."

"What?" she breathed.

"A goodbye," he said simply.

Her heart cracked open.

A goodbye not of abandonment—
not of separation—
but of release,
completion,
gentleness.

He took her hands again and guided them to his chest, where his heart would have beat in life.

"I do not belong in your present," he said. "And you do not belong in my past. But now we stand in a place between, where the soul can speak freely."

His eyes shone with unshed tears.

"And I want to give you what time stole from us."

He leaned forward and kissed her forehead—
a kiss full of love,
full of grief,
full of everything they never said.

She trembled violently.

"Leonardo... I don't want to leave you again."

He smiled softly, his thumb brushing her cheek.

"Mina... you already left me a lifetime ago. And yet, here you are. So this time, you are not leaving me."

He placed her hand over his heart again.

"You are carrying me with you."

She broke.

Completely.

He held her as she sobbed quietly, stroking her back, whispering into her hair:

"My love… my muse… my unfinished story… this moment is ours. And it always will be. But your path continues in a world where I am no longer needed."

She shook her head.

"You are needed. You always were."

He cupped her face in both hands.

"And now Leon is the one who needs you."

Her breath halted.

Leon.
Her Leon.
The Leon who lived in this century.

Leonardo continued:

"He is the continuation of my soul. And you… are the continuation of yours. You were never meant to look back forever."

She trembled.

He pressed his forehead to hers.

"I love you," he whispered. "I loved you then. I love you now. But love is not possession. It is release."

Her tears returned, softer now.

"And so I give you this…"

He held her cheek, his thumb wiping the last of her tears.

"…a goodbye that frees you."

A golden light began to fill the room again.

She clutched his hand desperately.

"No—please—just one more moment—just one more breath—"

He kissed her hand.

"You have a whole lifetime waiting for you," he whispered. "Go to it."

The light brightened.

His voice softened to a final, breaking whisper:

"Addio, anima mia."

Goodbye, my soul.

The light swallowed him gently—
not tearing him away,
but letting him fade like morning mist rising into the dawn.

Mina reached toward him desperately—

"Leonardo!"

—but her fingers closed on light, not flesh.

And the studio dissolved.

She fell forward—
into arms that caught her immediately.

"Mina! Mina—!"

Leon held her tightly as she collapsed against him, sobbing into his chest.

He whispered into her hair:

"I've got you. I'm here."

Her voice broke into his shoulder.

"H-he said goodbye."

Leon closed his eyes, holding her as if anchoring her soul in this lifetime.

"Then he set you free," he whispered.

She clung to him, shaking uncontrollably.

And behind them, the forbidden portrait glowed softly—
not incomplete,
not broken,
fully alive.

The painted hands
had finally touched.

208